GUNFIRE

——AT——

TWIN CREEKS

DAVID OSBORNE

Order this book online at www.trafford.com
or email orders@trafford.com

Most Trafford titles are also available at major online book retailers.

Printed in the United States of America.

ISBN: 978-1-4669-6809-7 (sc)
ISBN: 978-1-4669-6811-0 (hc)
ISBN: 978-1-4669-6810-3 (e)

Library of Congress Control Number: 2012921117

Trafford rev. 12/10/2012

 www.trafford.com

North America & international
toll-free: 1 888 232 4444 (USA & Canada)
phone: 250 383 6864 ♦ fax: 812 355 4082

CHAPTER ONE

For two days now the rider had seen no other traveler, not even a solitary cowhand or a lonely Indian. The temperature had been hotter than normal with no hint of rain and no breeze to speak of to cool down men or animals. His name was Morgan Reeves, he was thirty-one years old, standing two inches over six feet tall with wide shoulders and slim hips. His hair was black and his eyes were icy deep blue. His chiseled features were deeply tanned and tough as leather. By his side he carried a Navy Colt in a tied down holster and a Henry .44 rifle in the scabbard on his saddle.

His appearance would be described as unkempt due to the fact that his beard and the hair on his head had escaped a barber chair for the last several weeks. When he took off a sweat-stained brown hat to wipe his brow the long dark hair was unveiled. Reeves, was a quiet man who had a troubled past. He knew where he was from but he had no idea where he would land in the near future.

He dismounted and was walking his tired roan horse through unfamiliar country. He was doing it partly because he was tired of sitting in the saddle and partly because the horse was obviously tired of carrying him. Reeves did the usual things a smart man in unfamiliar territory would do to stay alive. He kept his careful eye on where he was going and also on his back trail where he had been. He watched for Indian signs, and made sure not to expose himself or his big roan horse to undesirables while riding the skyline.

Along about dusk, Morgan found his way onto an oft used trail. He halted the roan at a crossroads and looked around in all directions trying to figure out which direction he should ride. He took his canteen from the saddle and took a deep swallow of the warm water that he had been carrying since his last water hole. It wasn't much but that was all that he had left. He poured the remainder of it into his hat and allowed the big roan to drink as much as he liked. Morgan had owned the roan for several years and he had broken the horse to ride but he was still a spirited animal. He was a gelding with three white stockings and a star on his forehead. Morgan had named him Blaze. After the horse drank the water Morgan patted him on the nose and the horse tried to nuzzle his hand. "Don't have anything for you to eat you moocher." After several minutes of talking to the horse he mounted and turned the horse south, following a trail hoping to find a small town or a ranch where he could rest a spell and get some grub.

Morgan had been on the trail for several weeks and he was looking foreword to resting, a hot meal, a bath and a soft bed for the night. In fact he thought that if he found the right place he may stay a few days before heading out again. If the food was good enough and the bed was comfortable enough he would be glad to spend some time in a peaceful town.

After riding south for some time he had just about given up hope of finding a place to eat and sleep. He had resigned himself to sleeping in the open air another night but then he got lucky. Instead of finding a town however, he came upon a weather beaten old wood frame house that looked as if it might have once been a ranch house. Despite the battered condition of the building—loose and broken boards on the porch, shattered windows covered by cardboard, and a roof that looked like it probably leaked—there were horses tethered out front at the hitch rail. He looked up at the roof and saw smoke wafting from the old dilapidated chimney. His senses were peaked when he smelled what he thought was real food cooking inside.

He casually took out a sack of Bull Durham from his vest pocket, rolled a cigarette and lit it. He took a drag and replaced the tobacco in his pocket, broke the match and dropped it on the ground. He studied the building as he enjoyed the cigarette.

Morgan could hear nothing from the house or even the tied down horses from this distance. He rode a little closer to the building and then he could hear loud, coarse laughter, punctuating the stillness of the night. "This can't be an outlaw hide-out, being as it is on an oft traveled road. It also ain't no place for a café either," he mused as he sat atop the big roan wondering if he should stay around and try to get some food or play it safe and ride out in a different direction. Finally his weary bones, hunger and the smell of cornbread helped him make up his mind. With a quiet, "What the heck," he spoke to the horse and moved even closer to the building and hollered out, "Hello the house."

The big roan snuffled and tugged at the bit in his mouth. Morgan eased on the reins a little bit and the horse calmed down. He hollered again, "Hello the house."

There was a sudden quietness inside the house then a gruff voice yelled back, "Who's out there?"

He threw away his cigarette and answered, "Name's Reeves, Morgan Reeves, just passing through. I'm a stranger, you don't know me."

"You are right, we don't know you. I'd suggest that you move on," answered another gruff voice.

"I've been riding a long spell now. I'm tired and hungry; I won't give you any problems. I'll be riding out early in the morning," Morgan replied.

"What do you want?" came back the voice from inside.

"Like I said, I'm just looking for a brief rest for myself and my horse and a meal," answered Morgan.

He could hear some murmuring inside and Morgan was beginning to think that he was not going to be welcome inside, but then a loud drunken voice spoke. "So you're a stranger around here. Where are you coming from?"

"I've been most all over."

"That's not a good answer," the voice replied.

"I'm lately from around Masonville."

After several silent minutes the voice spoke again, "I guess you are okay, come on ahead, this may be your lucky day."

CHAPTER TWO

Morgan rode on up in the darkness to where the other horses were tethered. A tall, heavyset ranch hand with a long angular face walked out onto the porch and stood watching him. He had a half empty whiskey bottle in one hand a piece of meat and bread in the other.

"Look's like there are plenty to eat around here," Morgan said causally as he dismounted.

The man with the bottle stared at Morgan through the light from the door and just grunted.

"I'm gonna take care of my horse before I come in." Morgan smiled at him pleasantly and added, "Wanna give me a hand?"

The big man took a long pull from the bottle. "You ain't funny, Mister," he snapped. "And if it were up to me I would say that you are not welcome to come in." Then he turned on his heel and walked back inside the house.

Instead of tying Blaze to the hitch rail Morgan took the reins of the roan and led him a few yards to the barn. Once inside he slipped the saddle off and hung it on the wooden fence separating the stalls. A lantern provided enough light for him to find some grain. A couple of minutes later he was surprised to see a young boy coming into the barn carrying a bucket of water and a brush. He walked directly to the roan without looking at Morgan and he said, "You can go in I'll take care of your horse."

"Well thanks, Boy," he replied politely, "but I'll stay out here and give you a hand."

The boy stared at Morgan for a moment then spoke, "Suit yourself. You stayin' long?" he asked with anger in his trembling voice.

"Nope, just long enough to help you brush down this critter and get him some grain and of course some food for my empty belly. I've been riding him several miles and he deserves some rest and care. Most likely I'll be leaving early in the morning."

The boy didn't say anything but he stared at Morgan with a sullen look. Morgan looked back at him for a moment wondering what his problem was but then he decided whatever it was it wasn't his problem. Besides, he had his own problems. He scowled and roughly took the bridle off his horse and slung it on the fence with the saddle.

The kid quietly walked around the roan's side and began brushing. Morgan, now feeling surlier himself tossed the saddle blanket down at the far end of the barn. He figured that due to the size of the house and the number of horses tied at the rail he would probably have to sleep in the barn if they would even allow him to stay.

He looked at the boy, "Make sure that he gets enough to eat and that he gets plenty of water. And don't rub his back legs, because he hates to be tickled. And if he puts his ears back, get the hell out of the way."

The boy listened until Morgan was finished and said without much enthusiasm, "I'll tie him up after I get finished."

"No, just let him go, he'll stay around the place."

"He's your horse; I hope that you know what you're doing," snapped the boy.

Morgan didn't say anything but started toward the house. It was fully dark now and as he reached the steps of the porch he stumbled on the top step. He caught himself on the rail before he could fall. The front door was closed and he felt his way over to it.

He hesitated in front of the door as the sounds inside became louder and louder. Morgan was always cautious in unfamiliar places so he checked the cylinder of his Navy Colt then slipped it back into the holster. As an extra precaution he stooped and felt for the knife that he always carried inside his boot. He was thinking about going back to the barn for his rifle but decided not to. He then stepped through the door and inside the lighted room.

His eyes fell upon six men sitting at a long rectangular table. It appeared that their meal was pretty much finished but they still had several bottles of whiskey, some full, some partially full on the table.

What Morgan found curious was that the server was a woman. But she was not just any woman she was a very attractive woman. In fact she was one of the most attractive women that Morgan had seen in some time.

As he stood looking at the goings on at the table he noticed that the men all lowered their voices and stared back at him, while Morgan was sizing them up. What they saw was a man over six feet tall and about one hundred ninety pounds, every inch of him muscle and bones. Because of the sun and wind he had a weathered face so it was hard to tell just how old he was. He stared back at the men with a cold and trail hardened calmness that made some of the men shiver even though some of them were near the drunken stage.

It was probably only a few seconds but it seemed like hours that they faced each other. As time went by the tensions mounted and the possibility of violence increased because these men seemed strangely on edge. Morgan was not looking for trouble and he didn't quite know exactly what to think of this situation.

The tension was eased by the woman. "Howdy, Stranger, come on over and sit down. You boys make room." The woman looked at the men, "Joey, Pete scoot over and give the man some room," she said sternly. Surprisingly, the two men moved over leaving some space for Morgan.

"Mister, there are chairs on the wall. Get yourself one and pull it up to the table. Say hello to Joey Holgram, Pete Cordell, Jack Coleman, Willie Tackett, Wade Cross and Dusty Metcalf," the woman said to Morgan without any facial expression.

"We call that one Big Jack," laughed Wade Cross as he pointed at Jack Coleman. "You couldn't tell by his size though could you?"

Some of the men laughed nervously and all of the men except Willie Tackett nodded and mumbled greetings to Morgan. When they were finished he did what he was told and picked up a chair from the wall and moved it to the table. He took a second look at the man they called Big Jack and he understood why they nicknamed him. He was at least two inches taller than Morgan and out-weighed him by at least fifty pounds. Big Jack sized up Morgan quickly and then turned back to the other men. Morgan's thoughts were interrupted.

"I guess that you will want to eat first," said the woman with feigned indifference.

At first Morgan was not sure what she meant and started to ask her to explain. Before he could speak the men around him laughed and then pointed toward the woman and he understood.

His face was flushed as men continued to have a good laugh at Morgan's expense. Finally he sat down on the chair and only had to wait a few moments before the woman brought him a plate heaped high with steak and potatoes. On another plate were two large square pieces of the cornbread that he had smelled outside.

"I don't supply the whiskey. If you want any you'll have to bring it yourself," the woman said as she set the plates down.

"That's okay. I'm not interested in whiskey, how about some black and strong coffee, if you have some?" replied Morgan.

"Fine with me," she replied as she walked away.

Morgan kept his eye on her until she disappeared into the kitchen. She was indeed an attractive woman even up close but she was not as young as he first surmised. He guessed her to be maybe thirty or so. Her black hair was long and her eyes were brown. She was tanned on her face and arms so at least she spent some time outside rather than on her back. He also noted that she was perspiring freely from the heat of the stove making the loose fitting white cotton blouse she wore stick to her shapely breasts, outlining her figure for all to see.

She came back carrying a cup and a pot of coffee. She poured him a cup and set it down on the counter in front of him. She set the pot on the back counter and announced, "six dollars and seventy five cents. You'll have to pay in advance."

Morgan was taken aback, "I'm sure that the food is mighty tasty," he said, "but that is a lot of money for a meal."

The men guffawed and snickered and the woman glared at them. Her stare quieted them down and she looked back to Morgan.

"Look, Mister, for what you came for, the cost is six dollars and seventy five cents. Now I have to get my son to bed in the barn and clean up this place so that I can take care of my business."

"Ma'am, I'm sorry to bother you and the food is great but all that I want to pay for is the food, and get out of here. Now how much for just the food?"

She stared at him for a moment. Morgan was half expecting her to get angry or be annoyed with him but she didn't. She actually smiled at him for the first time and said, "Seventy-five cents for the food and you can help yourself to more coffee behind the counter."

Morgan took out some coins from his pants pocket and laid them on the counter. She looked at the coins on the counter and her smile disappeared and it was replaced with that same sullen expression that he had seen on the boy outside.

Evidently, she had him pegged as a broke and down on his luck drifter and that was the reason he was not interested in staying for the later doings.

She scooped up the coins and walked toward the kitchen. When she got to the door she turned around and announced that she was going to have a bath and that she would be ready for the men in about an hour after she got her son to sleep.

One of the men hollered at her, "Who's first?"

Morgan turned to look at the tall slender man with a drooping mustache over his lips.

"Not you, Joey. Wade will be first, I reckon he was here first." She then disappeared into the kitchen.

After she left, Morgan finished his meal, helped himself to another cup of coffee and carefully kept his eyes on the men in the room. He got the impression that they were not just plain cowboys but maybe gun hawks. Some were still eating but most were laughing and drinking. Wade Cross was the man that Morgan met out on the porch when he first rode in. He was a big man with a small scar on the side of his face and he had a pushed-in nose like someone had hit him with a shovel. He had two guns tied down low indicating that he was a true gunman. Morgan noticed that the bottle that Wade had been drinking from was now empty and lying on the floor next to his feet. He also noticed that the young man named Tackett appeared to be out of place with the group. He carried a pistol but it was stuck inside his trousers rather than in a holster.

The conversations continued as they frequently sneaked a peak at the kitchen door. Morgan figured that they were anxiously waiting for the woman to return. The men had almost ignored Morgan figuring that since he was not interested in the woman he was just a no-account drifter without the price of a whore.

The bantering continued on mostly about the woman and their own prowess with women. "She is quite a woman even though she is a whore," said Pete Cordell with a wide grin.

"Hell, Pete, how would you know? I know for sure that she's too much a woman for you," snickered Wade.

"I'll give you something to snicker about," said Pete as he headed toward Wade.

"Cut it out you fools and keep your dirty talk to yourself," snapped Dusty.

"Dusty, let 'em go. She's just a whore and not worth you getting involved," replied Big Jack Coleman.

Morgan glanced at Big Jack. He was even bigger than he thought before. The name Big Jack certainly fit the man. He was probably about four inches more than six feet and weighed more than two hundred forty pounds and quite a bit larger than the man named Dusty. His face was fat and his nose was too long for his face. A lot of his weight was hanging over his belt. Like most of the men, he also had not visited a barber for a haircut or shave in some time.

"She is still a woman and she deserves better," growled Dusty.

"You are too soft, Dusty, maybe I need to rough you up a little and harden your skull," snapped Big Jack getting more serious.

"Coleman, when you think you can rough me up, just come on and try it. It may not be as easy as you might think," he replied harshly.

Morgan got the impression that the two men were not the best of friends. In fact he was not sure that if any of the men were friends.

"Awe, Dusty, we were just joshin'," said Wade. "Don't need to start a fight."

Just then Joey nudged the youngest man of the group, "How about you, Willie?"

Morgan had noticed the young man sitting a little away from the rest and he had wondered about how he fit in with the group. Willie didn't answer right away and Joey repeated the question.

"How about me what?" snapped Willie.

"Are you getting in line?"

"Just leave me alone, Holgram," hollered the young man.

"You can bet your last dollar that your father would be the first in line if he were here," replied Holgram.

"Don't you say anymore about my father," hollered Willie as he jumped out of his seat and put his hands on the gun in his pants.

"Don't you do that, Willie," snarled Big Jack.

"You can't tell me what to do, Coleman." You are a big mouthed bully but I'm not afraid of you," he bawled angrily.

"You are a weakling, Willie, just face it. I wouldn't waste my time with you," hollered Big Jack mockingly.

Morgan expected the two men to fight but then Big Jack backed away. Willie though was not backing away. He jerked a knife out of his belt that Morgan had overlooked when he surveyed the young man and held it menacing toward Big Jack. "I'll gut you like a hog," he cried stepping closer to Big Jack.

Just then the woman came in from the kitchen door and stopped close to the two men. "What is all the commotion?" she hollered over the noise in the room.

With lightning speed Willie reached the woman. He grabbed her by the hair of her head, jerked it violently and put the knife to her throat. "Tell me the truth you whore."

The woman was now terrified. "You are drunk Willie. What truth are you talking about?" she cried.

"You know what," stammered the angry young man.

"No, I don't know," she pleaded for him to let her go.

"About my father you whore."

Morgan looked on intently but it was none of his business, besides, at some point Big Jack or one of the other men would intervene.

"You better tell him, Carla," said Holgram with a snicker.

"Someone please help me, this is no joke," she screamed.

Willie struck her in the face with the knife handle and immediately a large bruise appeared on her cheek. "You better tell me or you are going to die," he hollered even louder and put the point of the knife under her chin."

"Willie, please don't hurt me," she pleaded.

Out of the corner of his eye Morgan saw the young boy from the barn come out of the kitchen with a rifle. He was struggling to hold the gun level and steady. The tears streamed from his eyes but he was determined to protect his mother. He hollered at Willie to leave his ma alone.

Willie ignored the boy and pushed the knife blade harder against her throat.

Morgan saw the blood ooze out of the puncture in the woman's throat made by the sharp point of the knife. He was now convinced that the men were enjoying the spectacle and none of the men were going to get involved. "Willie, put the knife down," snapped Morgan.

"Mind your own business," raged Willie. "I'm gonna kill her and you can't stop me."

Morgan was not sure whether the young man meant what he said but he was not going to take any chances. He pulled the Navy Colt out of the holster aimed at Willie and pulled the trigger. The bullet hit the young man in front of his left ear, tearing into his brain. Willie twitched one time, dropped the knife and fell to the floor, dead before he landed.

CHAPTER THREE

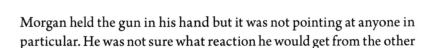

Morgan held the gun in his hand but it was not pointing at anyone in particular. He was not sure what reaction he would get from the other five cowhands, or gun hawks, whichever they were.

He looked at the boy. "Son, put that rifle down and go help your mother."

The boy glared at Morgan for a moment then dropped the rifle on the floor with a heavy clunk and ran to his mother's side. The woman, still sobbing, wrapped her arms around the boy and held him close.

"You okay, Ma'am?" asked Morgan without taking his eyes off the cowboys.

"How do you think I feel? I'm scared to death," she said between sobs.

None of the other men stirred or spoke but Morgan kept his eyes on them.

She dabbed her eyes with her apron and then wiped the blood from her neck, "I'm sorry, thank you, but you shouldn't have killed the boy."

"Maybe so but it didn't appear that any of your friends were going to help you out. They reminded me of vultures circling around waiting for the blood to flow."

"Unfortunately, they are not my friends, they are clients. I don't have any friends around here."

"Reeves, if that is your name, you are in a heap of trouble, in case you don't know it. Willie's old man is a big wig in these parts," said Big Jack caustically.

"I'll bet that Willie's Pa will pay a lot of money for capturing his son's killer too," growled Wade as his right hand slowly dropped to the colt on his side.

Morgan easily swung the gun toward Wade. "Yes, my real name is Reeves and my question is, are you planning on trying to collect the money, Friend?" asked Morgan icily.

Wade carefully moved his hand away from his gun and growled. "Newt Tackett is not gonna let you get away with this. I'd suggest that you quickly make tracks in the opposite direction of Twin Creeks."

"I'm not very good at running away from a fight, Mister," retorted Morgan.

"What are you gonna do now, kill all of us and keep the woman for yourself or are you going to hightail it out of here?" sneered Big Jack.

Morgan stared a Big Jack until the big man looked away. "You are not listening, I'm not planning to kill anyone unless I have to and I'm not planning to hightail it. As a precaution I want all of you gents to unbuckle your gun belts and drop them on the floor very carefully."

The man on his left named Holgram quickly lunged toward Morgan. Morgan could have shot him but instead he leaned back, then swung the butt of the Navy Colt catching the man on the side of the head. He sprawled on the floor in a heap like he had been pole-axed.

"Now, Gents, I've been riding for a long time, I'm tired, and when I get tired I get irritable, when I get irritable I do things I might not have done otherwise. Also, I have had to kill a man because you gutless no accounts would not intervene. So just do like I said before I get really angry."

The men looked down at Holgram and then unbuckled their gun belts and let them fall. "If you didn't have that gun pointed at me I'd rip out your insides and feed them to the hogs," said Big Jack.

Morgan ignored him. "Now move away from your guns very slowly."

Morgan could see the hatred in their eyes but he also saw that they had enough fear to keep them from doing anything stupid. He stepped closer to the woman and spoke, "Boy, go outside and get the rifles off the saddles of these men."

Startled, the woman asked, "What are you going to do?"

"Stay alive for the moment," he replied sarcastically, "Now Boy, go on quickly."

The boy looked at his mother and without waiting for her to say anything he ran outside. A few minutes later the boy came back with an arm load of rifles then went back out and got the rest.

"I brought yours back from the barn also," said the boy.

"Thanks, Son, that was good thinking," said Morgan.

"I'm gonna kill you, you bastard," snapped Big Jack.

"Unless you are going to talk me to death you're going to have to do it later because now you are leaving and taking your friends, including the two on the floor, with you."

Big Jack started toward Morgan and Morgan cocked the gun and pointed it at Big Jack's forehead. "If you want to join your friend on the floor, come on," he said.

Big Jack stopped and stepped back a couple of steps. "Now get started before I lose my temper," snapped Morgan.

"How and when are we gonna get our guns back?" asked the man name Pete.

"You got a town around here somewhere?" Morgan asked.

"Twin Creeks is down the road a couple miles," replied Pete.

"They got a sheriff there?"

"Yeah, but he will not be happy to see you," said Cross.

"That's too bad. I'll lose a lot of sleep about that. I'll drop your guns off at the sheriff's office when I get to town. If he is not happy, well maybe I'll just throw the rifles in the creek. Now, you two boys grab this body and take it to town with you. You Jack, help Holgram up and get him out of here."

Two of the men carried Willie out the door and the others followed. As they left, Big Jack, still helping Holgram stopped in the door and glared back at Morgan. "This is not over, not by a long shot," he said arrogantly.

Morgan glared back at him. "If I see you again tonight, it might be over quicker than you think."

Big Jack hesitated like he was going to say something, thought better of it, turned and walked out slamming the door so hard it shook on its hinges.

A few minutes later Morgan heard them riding out. He walked to the door and saw the five men riding south. One of the men was leading another horse with Willie Tackett's body.

CHAPTER FOUR

Morgan was sitting on the steps of the porch staring out into the blackness of the night. Only a few stars were visible in the sky. His mind wandered back to his childhood in Georgia and wondered how he had gotten from there to here. Since the death of his parents, he had no life other than that of a hardened fighting man. His mother died when he was fourteen and his father died while Morgan was serving in the Confederate Army. He got the word a couple of weeks after he died so he didn't even have a chance to attend the funeral. After he was mustered out of the army he went back home but it was not home. His only sibling was a sister that had married and was living with her husband in Waycross, Georgia. Morgan sold the farm and took half of the money to his sister and headed west. He had not been back to Georgia since.

He was startled back to reality when he heard the door squeak as it was opened behind him. He looked over his shoulder. There was just enough light from inside the open door to recognize the boy.

"Mister, I got some coffee for you. Ma said for me to bring it to you."

"Thank you, Son. By the way, what is your name?"

"Jamie, Sir. Jamie Jackson."

"Glad to meet you, Jamie, and thank you. My name is Morgan Reeves, please call me Morgan."

"Yes sir . . . I mean, Morgan, Sir. I just wanted to thank you for helping my ma."

"You are welcome. How old are you Jamie?"

"Ten, but I'm almost eleven."

"That was a brave thing you did," said Morgan. He wondered why the boy's attitude had changed so much since the encounter in the barn.

"I just had to help her, she is the only one I have now."

"Jamie, I just asked you to bring him coffee and not bother Mr. Reeves," said Carla as she walked out on the porch.

"Ma, I wasn't bothering him. He is my friend, his name is Morgan Reeves."

"Jamie I know who he is and you address him as Mr. Reeves," she replied sternly.

"Ma'am, the boy was not bothering me," interjected Morgan.

"I know that he talks too much but again I'd like to thank you again for your help."

"That's okay, Miss, uh . . . Jackson."

"Carla Jackson."

"Glad to meet you, Miss Jackson."

"And as for you, Jamie, it's time for bed."

"Aw, Ma can't I just . . ."

"Don't ma me, get going and wash up before you get in bed."

"Ma, can I sleep with you in your room tonight?"

The woman hesitated. "I don't know if Mr. Reeves wants to . . ."

"Morgan caught what she was going to say and interrupted. "Miss Jackson, I would prefer to sleep in the barn if you don't mind. I'll be leaving out early in the morning so I won't have to wake either of you when I'm leaving."

"Okay, Jamie, run to the barn and gather up your bedding and carry it into the house. And leave the lantern lit for Mr. Reeves."

"Okay. Ma," he hollered back as he ran to the barn.

"Mr. Reeves, I don't think that it is a good idea for you to take those guns to town tomorrow."

"Mrs. Jackson I have to. I told those men that I would drop off their guns. Also, I need to buy some supplies before I leave.

"Mr. Reeves, those men were right. Willie's father will see you dead if you go into town or maybe even if you don't. He won't rest until you are dead."

"Are you saying that none of those men will tell the truth to the sheriff when they get to town?"

Carla hesitated a moment, "Well maybe Dusty Miller but there is no guarantee that anyone will listen to him even if he does."

"Well, you know what happened here."

"Mr. Reeves, I wouldn't count on any man telling the truth and as for me, no one in town will believe a word that I say."

"Well then, why do you stay on here?" he said evenly.

"Don't try and change the subject. I know Willie's father, and he owns the general store and many other things in town. You would be crazy trying to get supplies there."

"There has to be someone in town that will listen."

"Willie's father will make sure that no one listens to you."

"I guess that I'll just have to avoid Willie's father while I am in town, and leave the supplies for later."

"You are not listening. Newt Tackett, Willie's father, along with Nick Baker owns everything in town including the sheriff."

"Miss Jackson, I gave my word that I would deliver those guns at the sheriff's office tomorrow and I always keep my word."

"Forget about your word, how about your life?"

The boy came back with his bedding. "Okay, Jamie, get to bed,"

"Good night Ma, good night Morgan."

"Good night, Jamie," replied Morgan.

When Jamie had gone through the door, Carla said to Morgan, "Good night Mr. Reeves and again I would urge you not to go into town tomorrow."

"Thanks for the warning, Miss Jackson, but I have to go."

"You are so bullheaded, just like all men. Go ahead and get yourself killed, why should I care?" she replied with anger, walked inside the house, slamming the door so hard that it bounced back and stayed open.

CHAPTER FIVE

Morgan wearily shrugged his tired shoulders and muttered to himself, "That woman is strange, but then again, it is her business and none of mine." He drained the remainder of the coffee in one gulp and looked around for a place to set down the china cup. He found nothing except the floor and he didn't want to set it down there. He got up, sighed deeply and knocked on the open door.

"What is it, Mr. Reeves?" she asked sharply.

"I just wanted to give you back your coffee cup so that it wouldn't get broken accidentally."

"Oh, thank you, there are so few pieces of the set left but I still treasure them. Was that all that you wanted to say? Have you changed your mind about sleeping in the barn?"

He ignored her insinuations, "I just wanted to apologize to you for the ruckus that I caused tonight."

Carla looked at him, "Are you sure that is all that you wanted?" she asked mockingly.

"Ma'am, won't you just let me apologize gracefully so that I can just get out of here?"

She waited for a few seconds then finally smiled, "Okay, Mr. Reeves, let's just forget everything and start over."

"Much obliged, Miss Jackson, I'll be going now. Good night."

"Mr. Reeves, are you really going into town tomorrow?"

"Nothing has changed; I still need to take those guns to the sheriff's office."

"I don't think that you should. I know all of those men in town and I know that they will cause trouble for you."

"I'm sure that you know them well," he snapped but immediately regretted what he had said.

Her faced reddened and her voice rose, "You can think of me any damn way that you want to Mr. Reeves, but I was just giving you some very good advice. Now if you'll excuse me I'm going to bed, alone."

She turned on her heel and started walking toward the bedroom. "Thank you for your advice, Ma'am, and I appreciate it but it is something that I have to do."

She continued walking without comment and Morgan just stared after her. When she entered the room and closed the door, he picked up his rifle turned and left the house. He stood on the porch looking out into the darkness and for a while trying to digest what had happened tonight. He pulled out his Bull Durham and rolled a smoke. He saw the light in the house go out so he headed for the barn. He put out the cigarette before he entered the barn.

Jamie had indeed left the lantern on in the barn and he found a straw bed that Jamie had used. He was tired so he stood the rifle up in the corner, unbuckled his gun belt, laid it down near his right hand then took off his boots. He curled up in his bedroll on the straw and after some tossing and turning he finally went to sleep.

CHAPTER SIX

Something woke Morgan suddenly. It took him a moment to figure out where he was. He lay motionless in his bedroll listening for any sound that didn't belong. He thought he heard a noise but he was not clearly awake so he ignored it and rolled over on his side closing his eyes. A few moments later he heard the noise again and this time he came wide awake. It was daylight. He lay still for a few seconds then reached over and took out the knife from his boot and held it ready. He got up on his knees so that he could see what was going on and he saw Jamie brushing Morgan's horse.

Morgan stood and the boy heard him and was so startled that he let out a whimper. Then he saw the knife that Morgan was holding.

"I . . . I . . . I'm sorry I didn't mean to wake you up," said the boy with a whisper.

"Boy, what are you doing sneaking around this early in the morning? You could have gotten yourself killed."

"I wasn't sneaking, Mr. Reeves. I heard that you were leaving early in the morning and I wanted to say good-by to you before you left," he answered with hurt in his voice.

Morgan dropped the knife back in his boot and stepped toward the boy. "I'm sorry, Jamie, I didn't mean to yell at you. I guess that I am a little jumpy from the events of last night and besides, didn't I tell you to call me Morgan?"

"That's alright and Ma said for me to call you Mr. Can I please stay in here a while? I'll take care of your horse." the boy pleaded.

"I'm sure that your ma won't mind if you call me Morgan and sure, Jamie, just make yourself at home. It's your barn."

"Okay, Morgan," Jamie replied.

Morgan reached down and picked up his boots and sat down on a pile of straw. "The horse is named Blaze."

That's a great name for a horse," said Jamie.

"Thanks."

"Morgan?"

"Yes, Jamie."

"Where are you from and why did you stop here last night?"

He reached in his pocket and pulled out his sack of Bull Durham, rolled a smoke and lit it. He took a drag and inhaled deeply before speaking. "Boy, didn't your Pa tell you that you don't ask a man out here in the west about his past? He might be a killer or robber on the run. Wouldn't you be better off if you didn't know and he just rode away?"

Jamie thought about that a moment and then replied, "Yes, I guess so, but I haven't been able to talk to a man since Pa died."

Morgan hesitated for a moment, "I'm sorry about your pa, Jamie. How did he die?"

"He was killed, a couple of years ago. I think that Ma knows who did it but she won't tell me."

"That is probably a good idea about you not knowing. I do know that losing your pa, especially that way, has to be rough. And to answer your question, there is not much about me to tell that you might be interested in."

"Are you a gunslinger? I like guns."

"No, I don't consider myself a gunslinger and any gun is a tool and nothing to play with."

"But you used your gun last night. Have you killed many people before last night?"

"Yes, I have killed several people, mostly during the war. It was my job to kill people. It was not something that I enjoyed doing but it was necessary. If I didn't kill them they would kill me. And I never lost any sleep over anyone that I killed," explained Morgan.

"What side were you on?"

"I was born and raised in the state of Georgia so I fought for the Confederacy."

"What was it like?" Jamie asked eagerly.

"Well, Jamie I . . ."

"That's quite enough," announced Carla from the barn door. I don't want you to fill my son's head with heroic tales of gunslingers and war heroes."

"But Ma . . ."

"Never mind, Jamie, you are much too young to hear those stories."

"Good morning, Ma'am," replied Morgan, unruffled. "I was just having a conversation with Jamie. No, I wasn't trying to glorify gunslingers or war heroes but it is reality and we all have to live with it."

"Jamie is only ten years old. He has plenty of time to learn about those things later," she replied softening her voice a bit.

"But Ma, I'm almost eleven and I was telling Morgan about my pa."

"That's okay Jamie we can talk a little later," Morgan promised.

She glanced at Morgan, "That is none of Mr. Reeves' business, now run along and get your chores done."

The boy paused for a moment and looked at Morgan like he was going to say something then he grudgingly left the barn.

"I made you some breakfast. You need to eat something before it gets cold and before you run off to get yourself killed."

"Thanks, Ma'am, that's very nice of you," he said as he dropped his cigarette and stomped it under his heel.

"Just come along before I change my mind."

"Yes, Ma'am," he replied and followed her inside.

He sat at the table in the kitchen rather than in the dining room where he had eaten last night. She sat across the table from him nursing a cup of coffee while he polished off eggs, bacon, potatoes and biscuits. He then washed it down with hot black coffee.

"That is a fine breakfast," he pronounced.

"I just figured that a man that is going to get himself killed should have a decent breakfast."

"Ma'am, are we going to rehash this same issue again?"

"No, I'm done. The rest is up to you. You appear to be a smart man so you make up your own mind."

"At least I thank you for that part."

They sat silently for several minutes without looking at each other or attempting to get up from the table. Finally, without looking at him she spoke softly, "I'm sorry about how I have talked to you and I really appreciate your help from last night. And I guess that I do owe you more than just the breakfast."

"Ma'am, you don't owe me anything."

"Please don't interrupt me. I want to finish this. I know what you think about me. But I am not just some cheap tramp that hops into any man's bed."

"Again, Ma'am, you don't have to explain to me. I ain't judging you. I have done many things that I should not have, so I'm not one to speak ill of anyone else. I'm sorry about that earlier remark."

"You were right about that remark so I can't deny it. I know that I don't have to explain but I want to. If you don't want to hear it then you can just get up and leave."

Morgan sipped his coffee and made no attempt to leave.

Carla went on, "My husband, Steve, was killed and he left this ranch to me and Jamie. Unfortunately, he didn't leave very much money. The few cows and some of the horses that he left were stolen soon after his death. I sold off the remaining horses except two and even that money has been gone for a long time."

She sipped her coffee and finally looked at Morgan. He looked back but didn't say anything.

"There is a mortgage on the ranch and I had to have money. I tried to get a job but no one would hire me. I tried to borrow money from the bank but the biggest depositor of the bank blocked the loan. Of course, he wanted to buy the ranch cheap and he wanted to bed me. He is the one who had my husband killed so there was no way I would sell the ranch to him or marry him."

"So you know who killed your husband?" Morgan asked gently.

"Oh sure, I know his name. It's Nick Baker and he is responsible for Steve's death. I think that everyone around here knows but no one will do anything about it."

"If you know who it is why haven't you spoken to the sheriff here in Twin Creeks?"

"Oh I have many times and like I told you before, the sheriff does what Nick Baker and Newt Tackett tell him to do. He has no time for me."

"I'm sorry about your husband, Mrs. Jackson, and the fact that you can't get any help."

"Well, you can see that we have all of this land and it is good land with plenty of water and grass. However, we were going farther and farther in debt and no way to get out. Jamie is a good boy and it is my job to take care of him, however I have to do it. I want him to have the ranch when he gets older and run it just like Steve would have. I don't like what I do either but it pays the mortgage and puts some food on the table."

"Ma'am, you have more guts than anyone that I know of but I also believe that by what you have told me, you are more bullheaded than I am," he said with a smile.

She was caught off guard by his remarks. She was not sure if what he said was a compliment or not so she didn't reply.

Morgan stood, "Thanks again for the breakfast." He turned and walked out of the house and to the barn.

Several minutes later he was saddled and walking his horse out of the barnyard. On one side of the horse was the bundle of guns that were securely tied to the saddle. Morgan wondered if Carla would come out of the house to see him off but she didn't. He also looked around for Jamie but he was nowhere to be found either.

He mounted, tugged on the reins of the roan and spoke to him gently, "Time to ride, big feller." He rode out of the barnyard toward Twin Creeks.

CHAPTER SEVEN

When Morgan left the ranch the sun was a hazy reddish disc barely clear of the tree tops. It had not yet lifted the mist that lay in the hollows. Dew lay heavy on the grass and the bushes. Somewhere in the distance a mourning dove cooed, welcoming the morning. Suddenly, a covey of quail burst from a nearby thicket. Morgan's head quickly snapped to the left, his eyes widened and his right hand dropped to his gun. He watched the birds flutter away and again he surveyed the landscape. There was nothing in sight and no sounds could be heard.

Several minutes later, as the big roan's shod feet hit the wooden bridge floor which crossed one of the two creeks just outside of town, there was a stir. A flicker crackled overhead complaining about the noise.

The ride to the town of Twin Creeks had been uneventful but by the time he reached town, the sun was now so hot that even the buzzards had quit circling the slaughterhouse just east of town. Instead, they were now perched on a limb of a tree nearby, with their ugly heads buried between black wings and only their beady eyes showing.

Being the county seat, Twin Creeks was a town of fair size insofar as towns in these parts were concerned. It not only boasted a main street but two others that paralleled it and two that intersected it. The population was growing steadily, heading toward five hundred people. Such was lost on Morgan since he was not given much to looking into incidental information.

As he rode down the main street looking for the sheriff's office he noticed that there were very few people in sight. Riding on he heard a noise off to his left. He dropped his right hand to the Navy Colt and looked around. It was just a mangy dog digging in the trash barrel behind the Rode House Café. The dog stopped and sniffed the air in Morgan's direction but then went back to digging for food.

He finally located the sheriff's office toward the far end of town. He guided the big roan into an alley that would provide him some shade and stepped down. He wrapped the reins over the hitching rail and walked around the building and up to the door. The door was locked. He rapped on the door and waited. Nothing happened and he rapped again, harder. Still, no one came to the door. Morgan turned from the door and looked out into the street, his brow furrowed with thought and some concern. He was not sure what he expected to happen but a knot grew in the pit of his stomach. Whenever this happened, it usually meant trouble. One of the reasons that he had been able to live this long was that he trusted his instinct.

He stepped off the sidewalk and onto the street, looked around, started toward his horse then retraced his steps down the street. It appeared that most every place was closed. Well, he was sure that one place would not be closed and that would be the saloons. He was wrong. The first two saloons he came upon were also closed. Fortunately there was a third, the Red Rooster Saloon, and it was open.

Morgan walked just inside the door and looked around. There were no customers and just and old grizzled bartender sitting at the table closest to the bar. The man wore a dirty white apron that covered his more than ample stomach. He was in the process of sampling his own wares. When he saw Morgan he hastily stood up, picked up the half empty bottle and stumbled behind the bar.

"Welcome to the Red Rooster, Stranger. I never expected any customers today," mumbled the bartender.

Morgan took another look around the room. There were six tables in the room and all of the chairs were stacked upon the tables except for the one that the old man was using. A crude wooden bar sat on the wall in front of the room. "I can see that," said Morgan with a wide grin.

"Want a slug of my finest whiskey?" the bartender asked.

"Don't mind if I do. I have a powerful thirst."

The bartender picked up a glass from under the bar and wiped it off. He then set it on the bar and started to pour from the half empty bottle.

"I think that I would like a drink from that full bottle over on that shelf," said Morgan as he pointed toward a bottle.

"What's the matter, you think I'm poison?"

"Nope, just would like a fresh drink but that dusty glass you have may kill me anyway," he retorted with a smile.

The old man looked at Morgan with a brief frown then his face quickly changed to a smile. He took a new bottle of whiskey off the top shelf, blew the dust off the bottle and polished a glass clean with a dirty rag before he set it on the bar.

Morgan gave him some coins and asked, "Town appears to be empty. Where is everyone?"

"They are all up on boot hill burying Willie Tackett. Say, who are you anyway?"

"Morgan Reeves, what do they call you?"

"Calvin Daniels, but the few friends that I have call me Cal. Where do you hail from?"

"I'm most recently from the Jackson Ranch a couple miles out of town."

"Mister, everyone knows where the Jackson Ranch is and by now they all know who you are. What in the world are you doing in Twin Creeks? You should be miles away from here."

"I promised some gents that I met last night that I would deliver some guns to the sheriff's office but his office was locked up when I rode in."

"It was locked up because the sheriff is out with everyone else at the cemetery."

"Okay, Barkeep, how about me leaving these guns here in the corner?"

"Suit yourself."

"How about you, why aren't you out with the others?"

"As you see, I'm an outcast in this town and I don't cotton to folks like Baker and Tackett. The boy, Willie, was a decent sort I guess but he was slow to learn. I'm surprised that he didn't get killed before now."

"Why do you say that?" asked Morgan.

"He was born slow in the mind and never got any better and he was also a hothead. Most folks around here backed away when he got mad because of his condition," said the bartender thoughtfully.

"Well, I'm sorry about what happened to him but it couldn't be helped."

"Mister, I understand, but saying you are sorry to Newt Tackett is not going to get you out of this mess. As I told you before, iffen I was you I'd git on that horse and ride as far as it will take you, and quickly."

"That is my plan as soon as I can get rid of these guns."

"You bring 'em in and be snappy about it. I'll pour you another drink for the road."

Morgan brought in the guns and stacked them in the corner by the bar. He picked up the drink that the bartender had poured and downed it in one large gulp.

"I'm hearing voices now, you better make tracks," said the bartender.

"Thanks, old timer."

"No thanks necessary, just git going."

By the time Morgan got out to his horse in the alley the crowd was coming back from the cemetery. He stepped in the saddle and started to turn the roan into the street. Someone called from the crowd, "That's him, git em'."

Morgan turned his head to see who had spoken and he heard a gunshot. He felt a heavy thud and searing pain before he felt himself falling out of the saddle. He momentarily blacked out but came round when he hit the ground. He tried to move but people were all around him. They were kicking him and hitting him all over. He tried to cover up his face but it didn't do much good. He could feel his ribs being cracked and blood oozing into his mouth. He blacked out several times and came to but the beating continued. Finally he heard the roar of a shotgun and then someone hollering. He fell into unconsciousness.

He didn't know how long he had been out but when he finally came to he wished that he hadn't. He tried to look around but his eyes wouldn't focus. Everything was a blur and his body ached all over. Some one was poking at him and then he heard someone speak. "Is he going to live Doc?"

"Don't know but with the all the cuts and bruises he would probably be better off if he didn't survive." He pushed on his chest and around to his ribs and Morgan yelled and tried to move.

"Yep, I'd say cracked ribs and those will hurt you for a long time, Stranger. I got the bullet out and bandaged the wound. It is not bad, it was a clean wound but you lost a lot of blood. I've cleaned you up some and I'll bind your ribs but not much else I can or want to do," said Doctor Colin Potter.

"I appreciate what you were able to do, Doc. I've got money I can pay."

"You might as well know, it was not my idea. I'd sooner left you lying in the street but the sheriff insisted."

Morgan was trying to understand what he was hearing. "I said that I got money, I can pay you for your bill."

The doctor moved away from Morgan. "I don't want your money, Reeves. You are a cold blooded killer and besides, the Tackett family is friends of mine even if the boy was not much good," replied the Doctor.

Morgan didn't respond but when the doctor began binding his ribs the pain was so great that Morgan blacked out again. By the time he came to the doctor was gone.

Chapter Eight

"Guess you are still alive, huh?"

Morgan groaned, turned his head and looked around. His eyes finally focused and he saw the bars of a cell and a middle aged graying man sitting in a chair next to his cot. "Why am I in jail?" he groaned.

"No other place to put you. The hotel wouldn't take you and I couldn't just leave you lying in the street to bleed to death. Although several folks advised me to just leave you there anyway."

"You must be the sheriff?"

"Yep, I'm Sheriff John Billings, at your service."

"I'm Morgan . . ."

The sheriff interrupted, "I know who you are, Morgan Reeves. Everyone in this town knows who you are. You are the feller that killed that boy Willie Tackett. That's the reason they wanted me to leave you in the street to die."

Morgan was having trouble breathing and he ached all over. His lips were cracked and swollen but he was still trying to talk. "Listen Sheriff, I did what I had to do because none of your good citizens would do anything. Besides from his actions I don't think that Willie was a boy."

"The town believed that he was a boy and keep in mind Reeves, none of these good citizens are going to take the side of a stranger or a whore against the son of one of our most distinguished citizens."

"Does that mean that the law only applies to the rich and powerful? If that's true the people who need the law the most cannot get it?"

"The town folks are law abiding people but they just plain don't like the doings out there at the Jackson Ranch. They got little ones and they don't want them corrupted. The town has new churches and they are preaching hell fire and brimstone and the decent women of the town are raising cane. In fact many folks think that she should be tarred and feathered."

"Let's see if I understand this. The men use her services and their wives don't like it. So why don't the wives just control their husbands?" he asked.

"You know better than that," replied the sheriff.

"Unfortunately I do and speaking of kids, of course you know, Billings, that Mrs. Jackson has a son out there also and he is a kid. What are you and your friends planning to do with him?"

"Billings nodded, I'm aware of the boy and I'm sure that so is Tackett."

"Sheriff, you're supposed to be the law around here. You have an obligation to keep her and her son safe."

"Look, Reeves, she will have no problem as long as she does what she needs to do."

"And what would that be?"

"She's finished here she needs to pull up stakes and move on. She and the boy can start a new life somewhere else."

"Sheriff, she's stubborn, you know that she won't leave her ranch."

"That would be a shame but I'm not going to put my job and my life on the line protecting a woman like Carla Jackson nor someone like you. I'd suggest that you move on and quick."

"Don't you believe that a man is innocent until proven guilty?" asked Morgan.

"I talked to the witnesses so I know you are guilty."

"Billings, you are a hell of a lawman and apparently a poor judge also," snapped Morgan.

"You can say whatever you want but no one wants this woman around and no one will defend her or you," exclaimed the sheriff.

"Apparently, a lot of men wanted her around considering the amount of company that she has had over the last several months."

"Don't start spreading rumors around town that may get you in more trouble than you are in now."

"Sheriff you know as well as I do that all of those stories are not rumors and how could I possibly get into more trouble than I am in now?"

"I got work to do, Reeves. I'm gonna leave this cell door open. I'd suggest that you be gone before I get back."

Morgan tried to shift his body but it was too painful. "Now how do you expect me to do that?"

"Not my problem and I can't protect you," he replied.

Morgan tried and finally was able to swing his feet off the cot. He tried to get up but again the pain was unbearable. He began to vomit and then blacked out again.

Billings picked up Morgan's feet and swung them back on the bed. "Have a nap," he said to no one in particular as he left the cell, leaving the cell door open. Stepping into his office he saw Carla Jackson standing just inside the door.

"Sheriff, I want to lodge a complaint," see said, her face flushed with anger.

"And what complaint would that be?"

"Some kids threw rocks at my wagon with me and my son on it. They were trying to spook the horse or hit us. Their mothers were with them and when I said something to the boys they cursed me and called me names and none of the parents intervened."

"I'm sorry about that, Mrs. Jackson, but I can't do anything about it."

"That's all that you can say, sorry? And you mean you won't do anything?"

"Yep, that's about it."

"So you are just like the rest?"

"What do you mean?"

"I think you know what I mean. Since my husband was killed you and the whole town have treated me like a leper. And of course you have made no attempt to find Steve's killer. I have had to take care of myself and my son without any help and you have allowed his killer to steal my cows and harass me. What else do I need to say?"

"If you are talking about Nick Baker, he is one of the town's most important citizens and you can't prove that he had anything to do about your husband's murder."

"That's your job to find the killer, not mine."

"Far as I know he is innocent and of course very influential."

"So that allows him to do whatever he wants to do with me?"

"I can't help you and I can't protect you so I'd suggest that you sell out, pick up your things and leave this area before someone else gets hurt or killed."

"You mean Willie Tackett, if you do . . ."

"Oh, yes him, but also the man that killed him."

"What do you mean?"

"That feller that killed Willie got shot and beat up pretty bad. Now, of course that could happen to you if you don't get smart, pick up your stuff and leave. You are a beautiful woman and I'm sure that you would make a lot more money plying your trade some where else. Now just . . ."

Carla interrupted, "What do you mean about Mr. Reeves," she snapped.

"Just like I said, he didn't get out of town fast enough so he got shot and some of the town folks showed their displeasure with him."

"Where is he now?"

"He's back in the cell. The hotel wouldn't take him, he was too bloody."

"I want to see him."

"I don't think you want to . . ."

She screamed, "I want to see him now."

The sheriff shrugged his shoulders, "Come on." He led Carla back to the cell.

Carla was shocked at the condition of Morgan. He was sweating profusely and his clothes were torn, tattered and blood stained. His body was covered with bruises and blood and he had vomit down the front of his shirt.

She looked at the sheriff, "What happened to him?"

"I told you. This thing could happen to anyone you know, even you. The doctor has been in and checked on him."

"The doctor, now there is another fine human being," she said bitterly. "I'm surprised that Mr. Reeves here didn't choke to death in his own vomit."

"He'll be all right and as far as the doctor, we all have got to do what we believe is right," he countered.

She could see Morgan groaning and moaning. "I'll bring the wagon around, help me load him in."

"Don't you have enough problems without getting involved with him?"

"Somebody has to help him and I'm sure no one in this town will do it."

"Okay. If that is what you want to do."

"I owe him that much anyway," she snapped.

"You know that no one else in this town will help you?"

"That's fine, I'll do it myself," she said bitterly.

"Okay, I'll help you get him on the wagon but that's it," he muttered.

CHAPTER NINE

Morgan Reeves became fully conscious but he couldn't figure out where he was and how he got into this bed. He smelled the clean sheets and then he remembered the blood stained sheets that he had been laying on the cot in that jail cell. "Well, at least the town will probably have to buy some new sheets and probably a new mattress for that bed in the jail. That may be some consolation."

He felt the cool breeze of an open window and turned his head. The movement gave him a headache but he decided from the sunlight it appeared to be late in the evening.

"Are you awake, Morgan?"

It took him a moment to recognize the voice then he responded, "I'm awake, Jamie," he said quietly. It finally dawned on him that he was back at the Jackson Ranch. It was an effort for Morgan to speak. His mouth and his jaws were sore and his chest felt like someone was sitting on him.

"Ma, Ma, Morgan's awake."

Carla came into the room. "Jamie, please don't shout!"

"I'm sorry, Ma, I was just telling you that he is awake."

"Okay, Jamie. Mr. Reeves, how are you feeling?" she asked as she put her hand on his forehead.

"How did I get here? How long have I been here?"

"Just be still for a moment and let me put some salve on your lips. They are healing but I'm sure they hurt a lot. Your fever is gone so you should be getting better soon."

"How long have I been here?" he repeated.

"Three days, do you have somewhere to be?" she asked sarcastically.

He tried to laugh but it hurt his mouth and chest and he had trouble breathing.

"Ribs are broken or most likely cracked. I rewrapped them tighter but they are going to hurt for some time. You may as well get used to the pain."

She checked the bandage from the bullet hole. "It appears to be healing nicely."

"Thanks, Mrs. Jackson but I still don't know how I got here."

"I found you in a jail cell and the sheriff was nice enough to help me load you on my wagon. Jamie and I brought you here and put you into bed. You had a high fever and you did a lot of talking."

"I have no idea what I would have talked about."

"You were talking about someone named Brandy, I believe," she said as she looked into his eyes.

He looked away, "I'm sorry to put you out like this."

"I guess that we are even then, you saved my life first."

"Mrs. Jackson, I think that you may have done much more for me than I did for you."

"Well, we'll just say we are even. I'm going to get you some soup. You need to get something on your stomach."

"Thank you, I think that I could eat something."

"Okay, Jamie you take care of Mr. Reeves while I go to the kitchen."

"Sure, Ma, I'll be glad to."

Five minutes later she brought back a bowl of soup and a slice of bread. "Can you sit up to eat or do I have to feed you?"

"I think that I can manage. Anyway, I'll do my best."

After struggling for some time he managed to sit up enough so that he could eat. The soup tasted good but it hurt his mouth. He was hungry so he managed to finish eating it anyway. The bread was too difficult to eat so he left most of it on the plate.

"Would you like another bowl?" asked Carla.

"I think that it would be better for me to wait awhile but thank you, Mrs. Jackson, again," he replied speaking with some difficulty.

"Well anyway, its now time for you to get some more sleep. We'll see you in the morning unless you need something before then. If so just holler."

"I doubt that I will be able to holler very loud but I'm sure that I'll be okay," he replied.

"I'll be sleeping just outside your door. If you make any noise I'll hear you," said Jamie eagerly.

"Thank you, Jamie. Good night, Jamie, good night, Mrs. Jackson."

"Good night, Morgan. Good night, Ma."

Morgan lay in bed for some time before he finally got to sleep but it was a difficult and painful night. He woke up around midnight and managed to get up out of bed. He felt on the table near his bed until he found his tobacco and matches. He thought maybe he would feel better if he walked and had a smoke so he carefully walked outside the house without waking up Jamie or his mother. He sat down on the porch swing, rolled a cigarette, lit it and stared out at the stars in the sky as he smoked. After several minutes he put out the cigarette, went back inside, got into bed and dropped off to sleep.

CHAPTER TEN

Morgan woke up the next morning when Jamie knocked gently while standing just inside the bedroom door. Morgan looked at him without speaking.

"Can I come in, Morgan?"

"Sure, come on in, Jamie," said Morgan.

Jamie walked up to the bed and looked down at Morgan. "You sure look better today than when we brought you here."

"Oh really! I must have been something awful when you brought me in then," he replied painfully.

Carla walked in the room. "Yes, you looked terrible when I first saw you in that jail cell. Your clothes were all ripped and you had blood all over you."

"As I remember, I felt terrible then too. Why didn't the doctor clean me up?" he asked.

"Mr. Reeves, the doctor didn't do much for you because of his hatred for me. The doctor and the sheriff are owned by Nick Baker and Newt Tackett. If they hate someone, the doctor hates them also," Carla replied sarcastically.

"So that's why he was so cross toward me."

"You are lucky that he was just cross with you. Do you want some breakfast?" asked Carla.

"That would be great, Mrs. Jackson. Thanks."

"I'll help you get it, Ma," said Jamie.

Jamie hurriedly left the room for the kitchen and Carla followed close behind. After they left, Morgan managed to sit up on the side of the bed. A few minutes later, Jamie came back with a plate of bacon and eggs. Following Jamie was Carla with a pot of coffee and two cups.

"The food looks good," said Morgan.

"I'm sure that you are so hungry that anything would look good. Sorry, I don't have any more flour to make biscuits."

"Yep, we are running out of food," added Jamie.

"You have no money or no one will sell you any supplies?" asked Morgan as he looked at Carla.

"You are right on both accounts. We have very little money and we are out of just about everything. However, no one will sell us anything for the few dollars that we do have. For the last few meals we have been eating whatever we could get out of the garden or find wild."

"I was afraid of that when I heard people talking about you and me in town."

"Enough about us and anyway, you are sitting up so you must feel some better," said Carla.

"I am doing much better," he replied.

"You are a man so you wouldn't tell me the truth anyway," she grumbled.

"I can't argue with that," he responded.

"I guess that you will be ready to leave soon?" she questioned.

"Morgan, you can't leave now. We need you," said Jamie.

"Hush, Jamie, we don't need to involve Mr. Reeves in our affairs more than we have already. I'm sure that he has other things to do and we don't want him to get hurt," she said.

"We can make that decision when we have to. Don't worry, Jamie," replied Morgan.

"Okay Jamie, go on. Get your chores done."

"Okay, Ma," replied Jamie as he rushed out of the room.

Carla picked up the dishes and headed for the kitchen. "I'd suggest that you get some rest."

"That's all that I have been doing is resting and sleeping. By the way, where are my guns?"

"I brought your horse with me. Your rifle is on your saddle and your pistol is in the other room. I'll bring it in to you later. I don't think that you will need it right away." She left the room, closing the door behind her.

Morgan laid back down on the bed and tried to go back to sleep but all he could do was doze a couple of times. Finally, he decided that he was going to get out of bed. After several tries he was up and on his feet. He had to hold onto the bed but he was up. The dizziness disappeared after a short while and be began feeling much better. He found his pants, they appeared to be clean but still had blood stains and some rips that had been patched. He assumed that Carla had washed them. He got them on and looked around for his shirt. It was no where to be found.

He figured that Carla probably threw it away. He looked in a corner closet and found a couple of men's shirts. They must have belonged to Steve, he decided. He put one on. It was a little small but it would have to do. He tried to pull on his boots but the bending caused the dizziness to return. He stretched out on the bed and tried to sleep. He must have at least dozed off because he got a start when Jamie ran into the room carrying his gun belt with his Navy Colt. At that time he heard a horse approaching.

"Morgan, Mr. Baker is here and I'm afraid for my Ma," cried Jamie.

"Okay, Jamie, don't worry. Here, help me get my boots on."

Jamie dropped the gun on the bed and grabbed Morgan's boots. He worked very quickly and soon Morgan had his boots on. Jamie grabbed the gun belt and handed it to Morgan.

"Shoot him, Morgan. Please."

"Hold on now, Jamie we can't just shoot people. I'll see what is going on."

Although Morgan had aches and pains he was fortunate that the gun shot wound had been on his left side rather than his right. He buckled the belt and tied down his holster. He then drew the gun, checked the cylinder and dropped it back into the holster.

"Hurry, Morgan. He's a mean man," hollered Jamie.

"Okay, I'm coming but I need for you to stay in the house. Stay down low and don't get close to the door or window."

"I'll be careful."

Morgan hobbled from the bedroom and though the living room toward the front door. He heard Carla talking as he walked through the living room.

"Hello, Mr. Baker, what brings you way out here?" Carla asked calmly.

"You know why I am here," he said without even bothering to say hello.

"I figured that you would be coming but I didn't think it would be this soon. I just turned you down for the fifth time a few of days ago," she said sarcastically.

"Look, I'm running out of patience with you. I want this land and I want it now."

"As I told you before, this land is not for sale. Not to you and not to anyone else. How many times do I have to tell you before you get it?"

"It don't matter how many times you say no, I'll get it anyway. My offer is two dollars an acre and that's my final offer."

Morgan slipped out of the door onto the porch and leaned on the wall without Nick Baker noticing him.

"Well, the offer was three dollars last time," she replied.

"Things have changed and you have fewer options than you had before. I'll buy it or take it for nothing."

"You are not going to do either unless you kill me first," she snapped.

"That can be arranged."

Baker slipped off of his horse and pulled out a knife from his belt. He stepped toward the porch.

Morgan took two quick steps even though they were painful and confronted Baker. "And just what do you expect to do with that knife?"

Baker was surprised to see him but he didn't back off. "Might have known you were here but you won't stop me."

He took a couple steps foreward but so did Morgan. "Drop the knife, Baker," he commanded.

"You are not going to do anything, there are too many people looking for you. They are going to hang you anyway," he snarled.

"If you don't drop that knife you won't be around to see anyone hang."

Baker stepped foreward and Morgan, with lightning speed drew his gun and fired hitting Baker on his wrist. The knife dropped to the ground and Baker howled.

"Now the next time you take a step toward her I'm going to blow out whatever brains you have in your stupid head. Now get on your horse and ride out quickly."

Baker hesitated for a moment while he pulled off his neckerchief and wrapped his bleeding wrist. "This is not the end," he shouted.

"It may be the end if you don't get on that horse and ride out of here. I'm losing patience with you."

Baker glared briefly at Carla and then Morgan. He quickly mounted and rode out of the yard at a gallop without looking back.

Carla turned and looked at Morgan, "You should be in bed," she scolded, "I can handle myself."

"Yes, It looked like you were handling yourself very well," he replied doubtfully.

He quickly turned to go back in the house, became dizzy, lost his balance, fell against the wall and went down on his knees. Carla gasped and rushed to his side.

"Mr. Reeves, are you okay?"

"I'm okay. It'll just take me a moment to get my bearings."

"Here, let me help you up."

Jamie came running out of the house. "I'll help too," he declared.

In spite of his initial objections he didn't protest very much when they took hold of him and helped him back into bed. "You are not well enough to be walking around so stay in bed," scolded Carla.

Morgan knew that he was fighting a losing battle so he lay back on the bed. "You are really pretty when you are angry," he said and tried to smile up at her.

"You don't know much about me. In my profession you don't have to compliment, just pay," she said bitterly.

"Mrs. Jackson you are not a professional, you are someone that has the courage to do whatever you have to do to take care of yourself and your son. I'm not going to pay you but I'll do all that I can to help you," he said.

She looked at Morgan and smiled. "That's a nice shirt that you have on."

"Someone got rid of mine so I needed a new or a different one," he quipped.

"I'm sorry I burned it. It could not be fixed or cleaned."

"Thanks for trying."

"I figured that you needed to have something to wear. Honestly, I didn't even think about my husbands clothes," she explained.

"Well, the pants didn't fit."

Carla looked him up and down as if it was her first time seeing him. "Yes, you are some taller and quite a bit heavier than Steve was. I'm surprised that you could even get in the shirt."

"It's a little snug but I can wear it for the time being."

She cast an admiring glance at him and shook her head, "Come on, Jamie. Let's leave so that Mr. Reeves can get some rest."

"Okay, Ma. I'll talk to you after a while, Morgan," said Jamie.

"You bet you will, Jamie," replied Morgan.

CHAPTER ELEVEN

Nick Baker rode to town looking for the doctor and quietly cursing Morgan Reeves. He knew that he would have been able to persuade or force Carla Jackson to sell the ranch if Reeves hadn't butted in. He had wrapped his wrist with his neckerchief but now it was bleeding again through the fabric. He had to stop and have the doctor look at it.

The doctor unwrapped Baker's still bleeding wrist and peered at it closely. "And just how did you get a gunshot wound?" asked the doctor.

"It's a long story," replied Baker

"How about the short version?" suggested the doctor.

"The short version is Morgan Reeves but I'm going to get even with him," he replied.

"Where did you tangle with Reeves?"

"At the Crazy J Ranch," he replied.

"Aren't you ready to forget that woman yet?"

"I'm ready to forget the woman but I'll never forget the ranch. I need it and I'll get it if it is the last thing that I ever do!" Baker exclaimed.

"Baker this may be the last thing that you ever do. This man Reeves will not be easy to take down," said the doctor.

"I've got a plan to get it done," he replied as he left the doctor's office and headed over to the general store.

This was the first day that the store was open after the funeral and Newt Tackett was behind the counter talking to a female customer. Baker walked up to the counter, "I want to talk to you, Newt."

"I'm busy with a customer. Can't you wait?"

"No," snapped Baker. "I can't wait, I'm in a hurry."

Tackett stared at Baker for a minute then called for his wife. When she came out of the back room he spoke, "Take care of Mrs. Winer, I need to talk to Mr. Baker."

The two men walked back into the storeroom and Tackett sat in a chair by the door. "Baker, what is so all fired important that it won't wait until I got rid of a customer?"

"It's what I can do for you, Newt. I'm going to help you get rid of your son's killer."

"And just how do you plan to do that?" he asked.

You know that your son's killer is staying out at the Jackson ranch with that whore don't you?"

"Yes, I've heard that but I can't do anything about it right now."

"Well, maybe the two of us together, along with your friends, can do something about it and get rid of both of them."

"What do you have in mind?" Tackett asked.

"You know that she is a blight on this town and an affront to all of the women here including your own wife. All of the decent citizens round here want to get rid of her."

"Sure, I know that no one in town will sell her anything or even talk to her politely. I'm sure that she will have to be leaving town soon."

"Newt, she is a hard woman to convince and with that killer out there with her, she may not be in a hurry to leave."

"You saw him and her out there? Why didn't you do something?"

"I saw her and him and he shot me without any reason," Baker added showing him his freshly bandaged wrist.

"Even with him out there she won't be able to eat and survive without help from the town folks and I'm sure that no one will help her."

"Starving her out may take a long time," explained Baker, "We are going to have to force her out."

"I know that you want her ranch and that you are in a hurry to get it. Why don't you just take your men out there and run her and him off?" asked Tackett.

"I admit I want the ranch but we both know that we all will be better off knowing that she is gone. However we need to get it done legally if we can," said Baker.

"Since when did you ever worry about the law or doing things legal?" muttered Tackett.

"The both of us can benefit with her gone and you know it. It will be better though if she volunteers to leave on her own."

They looked at each other, each wondering if they had guessed the real truth about the other and that woman. They couldn't know for sure but the doubts helped bind them together.

"I guess that you have a legal plan then, if you do I'm willing to listen," said Tackett.

"Newt, the town is ready to explode and the good citizens of the town are backing you all the way. All we need to do is for you to talk up the situation with the town folks. You tell them how good a boy your son was and don't forget to remind them how much you have helped each of them. The town folks will sympathize with you because of Willie so just don't let the issue of his death die down any time soon."

"What are you going to do while I'm riling up the town folks?" asked Tackett.

"I'll be working with the sheriff to make sure that everything is legal and I will be pushing that Jackson woman to change her mind. I'll be in touch with you later," replied Baker.

"What are you going to do with that whore?" he asked.

"Don't you worry, Newt. You just take care of your friends in town and I'll take care of her," promised Baker as he left the room.

§

"Mr. Baker, what exactly do you want me to do with that Jackson woman?" asked Big Jack.

"Jack, you can do whatever you want to do to her except kill her. And another thing, don't mark up her face. We don't want any sympathy from any of the town people."

"How soon do you want her taken care of?"

"No hurry, a couple of days would be good. Just camp close to the house and make sure that she knows that you are there. She may get nervous or afraid and decide to leave. That would be better for us if she would but be careful with Reeves, he may still be out there."

"I'm not sure I understand," he asked. "Why don't I just take care of Reeves for good?"

"Jack, I want her to worry about herself and that boy. I want her to be so afraid that she will be willing to sell the ranch or just leave it. Then I'll take it over."

"Well what if that Reeves fellar is still hanging around the ranch, what do I do?"

"I don't care about him. I'm sure that he will eventually realize that he is backing a losing hand and be riding out. Just wait awhile but if he doesn't leave voluntarily then we'll have to do to him the same thing that we are going to do to her."

"What if I accidentally kill her?"

"Well, that would be a shame, wouldn't it? But if it does happen, you better make sure that it looks like an accident."

Big Jack smiled, "I think that this job is going to be the most fun that I have had in a long time."

CHAPTER TWELVE

"Here have some more potatoes and carrots, Jamie. How about you Mr. Reeves, would you like some more?"

"I think that I have had enough. That was a good meal Mrs. Jackson, thank you very much."

"Ma, I'm getting tired of potatoes and carrots. We haven't had much else in a long time."

"Don't exaggerate, Jamie. It was only yesterday and I'm sorry but we don't have very many options as to what we can eat."

"How about you, Morgan, aren't you tired of having no meat and bread?"

"Jamie I'd love to have some meat and bread but the vegetables are good for you."

"Morgan, are you going to stay around for a while?" asked Jamie. "You said that we could talk later."

"We can talk but not now Jamie. I'm afraid that I cannot stay very long. I'll have to be riding out pretty soon."

Carla dropped her fork on the table, got up and left the room.

"Morgan, are you and my ma having a fight?"

"Jamie, sometimes adults just don't always agree about what is best or should be done. That's what is going on with your ma and me. We are not fighting we are just disagreeing."

"I sure don't understand."

"Neither do I Jamie. Sometimes women are difficult to understand. Say, Jamie, is there another town around here other than Twin Creeks?"

"Sometimes my pa rode over to a town called Sweetwater."

"Do you have any idea what direction and how far away this town of Sweetwater would be?"

"Not sure how far but sometimes he stayed overnight. I think that means it would be pretty far. He always rode west when he left the house."

"Jamie, get your chores done and don't bother Mr. Reeves," shouted Carla.

"Yes, Ma."

Morgan shook his head. He wasn't sure if Carla was upset with him for leaving or because he said he would talk to the boy later.

The day and night passed without much conversation between Morgan and Carla. The next morning Jamie walked out to the barn. The first thing that he saw was Morgan Reeves trying to put his saddle on the big roan.

"Are you leaving, Morgan?"

"Yes, I have to. How about helping me lift this saddle on my horse? My left arm is still a little weak."

Jamie stared at him for a moment then reached down and lifted the saddle up on the horse.

"Much obliged, Jamie."

"You are coming back, aren't you?"

"Don't think so, Jamie. I think that I've worn out my welcome here. Come over here and sit down for a moment," said Morgan indicating a bail of hay.

Jamie walked over and sat down. "But I know that ma don't want you to leave. I think that she needs you as much as I do."

"Don't you understand, Jamie? I have to leave for her sake. I have caused her enough trouble. Maybe if I leave everything will blow over and you two can go on with your lives."

"But, Morgan . . ."

Morgan put his hand on the boy's shoulder. "Let me tell you a story."

"Okay."

"Yes, I was in the war. I served over two years in places like Gettysburg, Cold Harbor and Shiloh. Places that I'm sure you have not heard of and I had never heard of before I became a soldier. I got a battle field commission and was mustered out as a major when the war ended. Yes, I killed a lot of people and I was wounded three times before I got out. The last time I spent three weeks in a Confederate Army Hospital. After I was mustered out I drifted west."

"What about your mother and father?" Jamie asked.

"My mother died when I was twelve and my father died while I was in the army. By the time I got the message of his death he had already been buried. I had nobody to go back home to."

"You lost your father just like I did."

"Yes, Jamie but you still have your mother who really loves you. I had no one. Anyway, the years went by and I moved around working at odd jobs and then found myself at a town called Masonville. I took a job as a deputy marshal. Some time later I became the marshal and I hired a young man as a deputy. We had a robbery in town and I took a posse, along with my young deputy, and trailed the robbers. We caught up with them, I made a big mistake and the young deputy was killed. I quit being a marshal and drifted again until I reached here. You see, I'm not a hero nor am I a gunslinger. I'm just an ordinary man trying to figure out what to do next with my life."

"I'm sure that you didn't mean for your deputy to get killed."

"No, that is true but it happened and it was my fault. I'm not someone that you or your mother could put your trust in."

"I just don't believe that you could do anything bad."

"Jamie can't you see I gotta go? Everything will be okay. With me gone it may be better for both of you," he tried to explain as he stood up and walked over to the big roan. He looked back at the distraught boy but couldn't find any words to soothe him. He struggled and finally got up on his horse. "Good-bye, Jamie."

The boy stood and waved, "Bye, Morgan. Hope I see you again."

It was difficult to leave the boy but Morgan turned his horse and rode out west toward the town of Sweetwater. His ribs were burning and he had a dull ache in his side and a bad headache but he had to keep moving, and he did.

From atop an embankment several yards away from the Crazy J Ranch, Big Jack Coleman studied the situation. The first thing that he saw was Morgan Reeves with his saddle bags on his horse and riding away from Twin Creeks. Reeves must have had enough and quit the territory. Big Jack decided that he would just wait awhile and see what happened. Big Jack was sure that he could take Reeves but it would be better if he didn't have to. Besides Baker had said that there was no hurry. He sat down with his back against a tree, pulled his hat over his eyes, and soon he was fast asleep.

It was going to be a long day for Carla Jackson. She had watched from her window as Morgan Reeves rode out and Jamie told her that he was not coming back. She cried a little but she was not sure why she did. She did know that she and Jamie had been alone for some time now and they could continue to do it longer if necessary. What she didn't know was why Mr. Reeves had just ridden away without saying anything to her. She realized that she had not been very friendly toward him but she had gotten him out of jail and cared for him. She finally decided that she had no business allowing herself to think about a man like Morgan Reeves anyway.

In the afternoon she went in and cleaned up the room that Morgan had used. She put new sheets and pillow cases on and left the dirty ones to be washed. She found that all of Reeve's things were gone. She was still hoping that maybe he would come back but now she was quite sure he wouldn't. This was the same room that she had shared with so many men that she couldn't count but she had not shared her bed with Morgan Reeves. "Damn him," she thought bitterly, "He is just the same as all other men." However, after thinking about it, she was not so sure.

She and Jamie finished their chores and got ready to fix super. They dug some potatoes and carrots and noticed that they were even running out of those. Although Jamie complained about the food she was more worried about when they ran out. What were they going to eat when the carrots and potatoes were gone?

Jamie helped her fix the meal and didn't even complain. She wished that she had some coffee for them but she had thrown out the over-used grounds this morning. The coffee was so weak it tasted like water anyway. They ate the food and washed it down with cold water. He helped her clean up the kitchen and stayed as close to her as he could. He was lonely and after she had put him to bed she decided that she was lonely also. She tried to think logically why she was feeling this way but only one answer came to her and she didn't want to think about that.

After walking around the house for some time she decided that she would try and go to sleep. She walked into Jamie's room, bent over and kissed him without waking him. She undressed, picked up a book from the book shelf and got into bed. She tried to read but she couldn't concentrate. She was still thinking about Morgan Reeves, why he had rode out and where he was now. She laid the book down on the table beside the bed, fluffed her pillow and tried to get comfortable. She was just ready to doze off when she heard a noise that caused her to sit upright in the bed. Not hearing it again, she lay back down. Then she heard another noise. She figured that it was Jamie getting up to get a drink of water so she got up and lit the lamp just in case he came in the bedroom.

Her bedroom door exploded inward and landed on the floor in front of her bed. Behind the door came Big Jack Coleman grinning from ear to ear. She knew immediately why he was here and she rolled out of bed on the other side and came to her feet. She tried to run pass him toward the door but he grabbed her by the arm and her hair and held on. She tried to jerk away but he swung her around, slapped her on the side of her head, knocking her backward on the bed. She struggled but couldn't get free.

Jamie ran in the door. Seeing what was going on he jumped on Big Jack's back. "Leave my ma alone," he yelled.

Big Jack reached around with one big paw and grabbed the boy by the hair of the head. He jerked so hard the boy come flying over Big Jack's head. He landed hard on the floor and cried out with pain. Big Jack kicked the boy in the ribs and cursed him, "Git out of here, Boy. I'll kill you if you don't git."

Carla reached out and raked her fingernails down his face and screamed, "Jamie, run, go get help."

Jamie, now on his knees crawled past big Jack through the bedroom door and got to his feet. He ran as fast as he could while looking back over his shoulder to see if he was being followed.

But Big Jack didn't care where the kid went; nobody was going to help him anyway. He grabbed Carla by her hair and jerked her up with one hand. With the other hand he grabbed her night gown and ripped downward. The buttons went flying and the gown came open. He jerked it off and tossed it on the floor and threw her back down on the bed. She screamed and screamed but Big Jack ignored her screaming. He slapped her across the face and hit her in the stomach with his fist over and over again. At first she screamed and then she blacked out. Finally Big Jack stopped hitting her. He raped her over and over again. When he was finished he left the bedroom and went into the kitchen. He decided that he was really hungry. He searched the kitchen thoroughly but all that he could find was some raw carrots. He picked up a handful, took a couple of bites and threw them down. He ransacked the kitchen scattering things on the floor before he took his time leaving the house.

Chapter Thirteen

Jamie ran out the door crying. His nose was bleeding and his lip was cracked and his chest hurt so bad he could hardly breathe. In spite of the pain he decided that he had to get help. He thought about running to town but then he remembered the horse in the barn. He ran in, managed to put a halter on the horse and climbed aboard without the saddle. He dug his heels in the horse's side and rode as fast as he could into Twin Creeks. It was pitch black and Jamie was sure glad that the horse knew the way.

He slid off the horse in front of the sheriff's office and ran up to the door. The door was locked. He pounded on the door but no one came. He pounded again and again but no one came. He didn't know what he was going to do so he sat down on the porch steps in front of the sheriff's office. He cried and cried.

"What's the matter, Boy?"

The voice startled Jamie for a moment and then he raised his head and looked around but didn't see anyone. The voice spoke again and Jamie turned his head and looked around again. At first he thought he was imagining things when he saw a figure.

"You okay, Boy?" repeated the voice.

"I'm okay but I need the sheriff," he cried.

"The sheriff just rode out of town. Probably won't be back until tomorrow."

Jamie just stared at the man and didn't speak.

"I'm Cal Daniels. Can I help you?" asked the man as he drunkenly stumbled toward the boy.

"Someone is hurting my ma. I need the sheriff."

"Who is it?" asked Daniels.

"It was dark but he was really big, probably Big Jack," sniffed the boy.

The old bartender saw the blood on the boy. "Come with me boy, I'll try and clean you up."

"Mister I don't need cleaned up, I need help for ma."

"I tell you what, as soon as the sheriff gets back I'll tell him. Now come with me."

Jamie didn't want to leave but he reluctantly did because he didn't know what else to do. The old bartender took him into the Red Rooster Saloon and sat him down at a table. He took a white rag and a basin of water and cleaned the boy up. He took his bottle of whiskey and took several large swallows then poured a glass half full of whiskey and set it in front of the boy. "Drink up," he commanded.

The boy had never tasted whiskey but he did what the bartender told him to do. The whiskey burned all the way down but Jamie began to feel better almost immediately.

The bartender took the bottle and poured some of the contents onto the cuts on the boys face and neck. The boy yelled but then stopped.

"Now, Boy, get back home and do what you can for your mother. I'd go with you but I can't walk or ride and I'm too drunk to do anything else."

The boy wiped the whiskey off his face with his shirt sleeve and left the saloon. He found his horse and rode back to the ranch. He ran into the house and into his mother's bedroom. She was lying on the floor. Jamie bent down and tried to wake her up but no luck. He ran to the kitchen, got a wet rag and ran back to the bedroom. He cleaned her face up, got a pillow off the bed and put it under her head. He looked at the blanket but it was covered with blood. He ran to his room, got the blanket off his bed and brought it back. He covered her and then sat down on the floor and talked to her even though she didn't answer. Finally he lay down beside her and dozed off to sleep.

The next morning he woke up, picked up the rag and took it to the kitchen to wet it down again. He brought it back to the bedroom and placed it on her forehead. She moaned and opened her eyes.

"Ma, I'm glad that you are awake."

"Oh Jamie, Jamie are you okay?"

"I'm okay, Ma. How can I help you or what can I get for you?"

"Get me some water to drink and help me onto the bed please," she answered weakly.

Jamie ran to the kitchen and brought a cup of water. Carla tried to drink but most of it spilled on her and the floor. It took some doing but he finally got her up and on the bed. He picked up the pillow, put it under her head and covered her with a sheet and stood over her.

"Can you go get me some more water, Jamie, but this time carry it in a pail so that I can wash up?"

"Sure, Ma."

He went to the kitchen and got a pail of water and brought it back to the bedroom. She managed to sit up, covered herself with the sheet, took the rag, dipped it in the water pail and tried to clean herself up. She looked over at Jamie and took one of his hands.

"Ma, what are we gonna do? I went to town to get help but the sheriff was not there. The man said that he would tell him when he got back."

"Jamie, I don't think the sheriff will help us anyway, especially if he has to ride out here. Just do your chores and let me rest a while and hopefully I'll feel better after awhile."

But as the day dragged on she didn't feel any better. She tried to get out of bed but she ached all over and she became dizzy. She lay back on the bed and waited for the dizziness to disappear.

After he finished his chores Jamie pulled up a chair next to his mother's bed and watched her. She dozed off and woke up but she spoke very little except for requesting more water. The wind blew through the window and finally it started getting dark. Rough weather was blowing in. It started with lightning and loud claps of thunder and then the rain came. Jamie managed to get the window closed before the rain started. It rained hard for several minutes and then it slacked off but it continued to come down in a drizzle.

Jamie fixed some soup and tried to get his mother to eat some of it but she refused. He ate a little but he decided that he was not very hungry. He continued to put wet rags on his mother's forehead because she was burning up. He continued to talk to her but she either didn't respond or just moaned or groaned.

"Ma, you are gonna be okay. I'm gonna take care of you," he whispered but she didn't answer.

"Ma, Morgan is going to come back, I know he is. He'll help us when he gets back." At the mention of his name she perked up for a minute but then dozed off. After a while Jamie crawled up on the bed with his mother and went to sleep.

CHAPTER FOURTEEN

Big Jack knocked on Nick Baker's office door at the ranch house and then walked in. Baker frowned when he saw Big Jack but didn't say anything. He needed Big Jack to do a job but he still didn't care for the big man. Big Jack walked over to the table and picked up a bottle of Baker's best whiskey and poured two fingers in a glass. He picked up the glass and drained it in one swallow.

"Coleman, have you heard anything from that Jackson woman lately?" asked Nick Baker.

"Not a word. Not since I roughed her up a couple of days ago," he replied as he poured himself another drink.

Baker was irritated as he picked up a cigar from his desk and chewed off the tip. He stuck it in his mouth and chewed on it a minute then struck a wood kitchen match to the end and it flared up.

"Do you think that you might have killed her?"

"I don't think so, she was still breathing when I left her. The boy went to town and stopped off at the sheriff's office but Billings was out of town."

"I heard that too. I spoke to the sheriff and I'm sure that he would know better than to get involved. He likes that badge and wants to keep it for a while."

"I agree, he should know better than to help her out. Maybe she woke up and decided that she best pack up and git herself and the boy out of the territory."

Baker did not believe that for a moment but he was worried about something else. "Are you sure that Reeves feller has pulled out for good?" he asked while rubbing his sore wrist.

"I'd say that he is gone. He had his saddle bags and he rode out away from town. Sure looked like he wasn't coming back."

Baker puffed on the cigar, "In a way I think that his leaving is too bad. I'd sure like to see him get his just due."

"He's a tough customer. You might want to just let him go quietly."

"Anyway, Jack, I think that you need to stay away from town and the Jackson Ranch for a while. I don't want for you to get in trouble now. Take a couple of the boys and move into the southwest corner line shack. I'll send for you when I need you."

"Boss, I can take care of myself. If I get in trouble I can get myself out."

"Maybe so, but I can't take a chance."

"Okay, Boss, I'll be around when you need me."

§

Jamie awoke early and heard someone in the house. He got out of bed and carefully made his way into the kitchen.

"Morgan, I'm glad you are back," he sobbed as he ran to him.

Morgan took the boy in his arms and held him close. "Is something wrong?"

"Its ma, she's hurt really bad."

"Where is she now?"

"She's in the bedroom."

"You finish putting these supplies away and I'll look in on her."

"Okay. Morgan. I'm sure glad that you are back."

Morgan smiled at the boy and then walked into the bedroom and saw Carla curled up on the bed. He checked her forehead and she was still hot. He touched her and whispered to her and she slowly opened her eyes.

He bent down close to her, "Everything will be okay now. I'm gonna take care of you."

"Morgan . . ." that's all that she could get out.

"Hold on, I'll be right back."

He went to the kitchen, got a fresh pan of water and a washcloth. "Jamie, get a glass of water for your mother."

Morgan took the pan and went back to the bedroom. He lifted the blanket and saw that Carla was completely naked. She had scratches and bruises almost all over her body and she still had dried blood from her wounds. He poked the bruised areas gently but there didn't appear to be any broken bones. He took the wet rag and cleaned her from top to bottom. After that he turned her over on her stomach and completed the clean up. She had bruises on her back also but nothing serious.

He found her torn nightgown and got it on her. She was now awake but still dazed. He propped her up and Jamie gave her the glass of water. She drank most of it only stopping to rub her bruised lips.

"Jamie, you take care of your ma and I'm going to fix something to eat for you and your mother."

"Morgan."

"Yes, Jamie."

"Can we please not have potatoes and carrots today?"

Morgan smiled but didn't reply. He went to the kitchen and made coffee. A short while later he had soup fixed for Carla and bacon and eggs for Jamie. He took the soup and two cups of coffee to the bedroom.

"Jamie your meal is in the kitchen, and there are no potatoes or carrots."

"Oh goody," replied Jamie as he ran out of the bedroom.

Morgan set the coffee down on the table then sat down on the side of her bed. "Let me feed you some soup."

"Good, I don't know if I can feed myself."

Within the next few minutes, with Morgan's help, Carla had eaten all of the soup and drank most of the coffee. "The only thing that I can say is thank you, Mr. Reeves. I just don't know how to thank you properly."

"Well, you took care of me when I was hurt and now I guess it is my time to take care of you," he said with a smile.

"Okay, we'll just call it even."

"Now I want you to rest and I'll bring you more soup and coffee after awhile."

"There are clean sheets in the closet; can you change them for me?"

"Absolutely, I'll be glad to." He got the sheets, helped her out of bed and into a chair then he changed the sheets.

"Can you also get my other night shirt in the back of the closet?"

He found the night shirt and handed it to her. After trying to raise her arms over her head and couldn't, she asked Morgan to help her.

"Ma'am, I don't know about that . . ." he stammered.

She smiled at him, "Mr. Reeves, you have seen me without my clothes. I have nothing left that you have not seen."

"But that was when you were hurt."

"I'm still hurt and I still need help, please," she pleaded.

He hesitated for a moment keeping his eyes down toward the floor. "Okay, reach your arms straight out in front of you."

She was standing in front of him naked and Morgan tried his best to ignore her perfectly shaped breasts, bruised though they were. He held out the night shirt and Carla slipped her arms through the sleeves. He then found the hole for her head and slipped it over, allowing it to fall below her knees.

She thanked him politely and blushed when their eyes met.

"Glad to do it." He helped her back into bed, turned his head away and covered her with the sheet. "I'll get you some more coffee."

"Wait, I think that I will take a nap. You can wait for the coffee but can you come closer to the bed?"

"You are welcome, Mrs. Jackson, and I'll be glad to come closer."

She reached out and took his hand, "Thank you kindly, Mr. Reeves."

"You are most welcome, Mrs. Jackson. Now try and rest," he replied with a smile and squeezed her hand gently. She smiled slightly then turned over and soon she was sleeping.

Morgan went into the kitchen to check on Jamie. The boy had finished his meal and put away the remainder of the supplies into the cabinet. "Jamie, I'm going out to the barn. If your mother needs me, holler."

"Okay, Morgan. Do you need any help?"

"No, Jamie, I'm just going to take care of my horse."

As he headed toward the barn, several thoughts were running through his mind. Morgan knew what he had to do but he didn't want to leave Carla and Jamie alone right now. "This job will have to wait and I'm going to enjoy every minute of it," he told himself.

After taking care of the big roan, Morgan completed some needed repairs on the barn and the corral. Even though he was busy the morning went slowly but soon gave way to afternoon. Carla slept a lot and Jamie took a couple of short naps. Morgan fed her some more soup and sat down and watched her as she slept. Yes, he knew what he had to do. He was going to find the man that beat up and raped Carla and kill him and he was pretty sure that he already knew who he was.

After supper he put Jamie to bed and tried to sleep. Many things kept going through his mind. If in fact Big Jack was the one who beat up and raped Carla, he was going to have a lot of friends from Nick Baker's ranch and the local town folks. While he had been in Sweetwater he had sent a telegram to his friend Tom Clay in Masonville but that was far away from here. And of course, he was not sure that Tom would ever get the message or even come if he did.

Some time later that night he went off to sleep. He didn't wake up until the next morning when Jamie came in and shook him. Morgan reached for his gun but recognized Jamie. "What are you doing waking me up?"

"Morgan, I'm hungry and so is ma."

He rolled over and sat on the side of the bed. "How is she doing?"

"She is awake and talking and she said she was hungry and that I should wake you up."

"Feisty, huh? Okay Jamie lets fix her some breakfast."

Morgan slipped on his boots and followed Jamie into the kitchen. He washed up, combed his hair and started breakfast. A short while later breakfast was cooked. Jamie ate his in the kitchen and Morgan took Carla's to the bedroom where she was sitting up, waiting.

"Good morning, Mrs. Jackson. You look some better I hope that you also feel better."

"Good morning, Mr. Reeves. I'm always thanking you for something, aren't I?"

"You can thank me by telling me who did this to you."

"Mr. Reeves, I don't want you get involved, I'll be all right in a few days."

"Ma'am, I'm already convinced that it was Big Jack that did this. You may as well tell me the truth."

"Yes, it was, but you need to ride out. I don't want to be responsible for you getting killed."

"Eat your breakfast and I'll be back to check on you."

"Mr. Reeves, please."

He walked out of the bedroom and into the kitchen where Jamie had just finished his breakfast.

"Are you going to go after Big Jack?"

"Is Big Jack the one who hurt your ma?"

"Yes, and he hurt me too. I went to town to get the sheriff but he was not in his office. Mr. Daniels fixed me up and gave me a drink of whiskey."

"He did, huh?"

"Yep. He told me he would send the sheriff out to the ranch but he never came."

"Jamie, I'm sure that Mr. Daniels gave him the message but the sheriff is not concerned about our problems."

"You'll get him, won't you?"

"Don't worry about it Jamie. Do your chores." Morgan ate his breakfast, drank two cups of coffee and headed for the barn. He saddled up and rode the two miles or so into Twin Creeks. He stopped and dismounted in front of the sheriff's office. He was quite sure the sheriff would be of no help but decided to try anyway.

When he strode inside he saw the sheriff sitting behind his roll-top desk with his feet cocked up and reading a week old newspaper.

"Well, Reeves, I'm surprised to see you back in town," he remarked without looking up.

"I'm sure that you are," quipped Morgan.

"I'm very busy, what can I do for you?" replied the sheriff indifferently.

"I can see how busy you are. How many times have you read that paper?" asked Morgan.

"I read it every day until the next edition comes out," he replied casually.

"Well, I got news for you that you don't have to read out of that paper."

"And what would that be?" asked the sheriff with a decided lack of interest.

"Carla Jackson got beat up and raped by Big Jack Coleman a couple of nights ago."

"Yes, Reeves, I heard that somewhere. That was really too bad, huh?"

"Don't you think it might be time for you to be doing something and earning your pay?"

"Reeves, I spoke to Big Jack and he has an alibi so what would you expect me to do?"

"That alibi wouldn't be Nick Baker, would it?" asked Morgan sarcastically.

"It would," said Billings with a cynical smile.

"You are the law here. That means you get at the truth, not just take someone's word that has an axe to grind."

"Reeves, that woman and child needs to leave this country if she knows what is good for her and I'd suggest that you go along with her. With you escorting her, you both can have a good time and the town will be rid of one whore."

With one swipe Morgan knocked the sheriff's feet off the desk, grabbed him by the shirt collar and yanked him to his feet. "If you make any more disparaging remarks about her I'll tear your guts out and stuff them down your throat."

"Look, Reeves, you had better take your hands off of me," he stuttered.

"Or what, you'll arrest me? That's not going to happen," he snapped as he shoved him back into the chair.

"I'm the law here . . ."

Morgan interrupted, "Now you are the law but with Mrs. Jackson you can't do anything." He backed up a couple of steps and put his hand on his gun. "Go ahead and arrest me," he said with a sneer.

"I'm just saying that it would be better for her to leave," he replied but he made no effort to get up or reach for his gun.

"Billings, you know that she is not going to leave the ranch and she is entitled to protection from the law," snapped Morgan.

"Damn it, Reeves, how many times do I have to tell you? She is not getting protection from this office and if she is too dumb to leave she deserves what she gets," he yelled.

"Billings, if anything else happens to her, I'm going to hold you personally responsible," Morgan replied flatly.

"What are you saying?"

"What I'm saying is that if you don't do your job, I'll do it for you and then I'll be back for you."

"You try and do that and there'll be hell to pay," warned the sheriff. But Morgan didn't hear him. He was already heading out the door.

There were several people around but Morgan ignored them and headed straight to the Red Rooster Saloon. It was mid afternoon and he was not sure if the saloon would be open. It was.

He walked in and saw Cal Daniels sitting at the same table that he was sitting in the first time Morgan met him. "Hello, Mr. Daniels."

"Well now if it ain't Mr. uh Mr . . ."

"Mr. Reeves."

"I drink too much and my memory is shot. I remember you now, young man."

"I wanted to thank you for taking care of the boy."

"Aw shucks, twarn't nothing, I just wished I could have done more. By the way, how is Mrs. Jackson?"

"He did a number on her. Where would I find Big Jack?"

"Mr. Reeves, why don't you take Carla and the boy and get them out of the territory?"

"Cal, you know that she won't leave and even if she would, someone needs to pay."

"How do know for sure that he was the one?"

"Because I asked her, now where is Big Jack?"

"Reeves, I don't think that you really want to find him. He is a mean ornery cuss."

"I know, that's why I need to find him. Now how can I find him?"

"Well, I was told that Nick Baker had him hide out to a shack a few miles out of town."

"Where is the shack?"

"It's on Baker's property and it would probably be well guarded."

"Can you give me directions to it?"

"Well, don't tell me I didn't warn you."

"I promise I won't hold you responsible."

Cal Daniels finally consented to give him the directions. Morgan had a drink with the old man, tossed some coins on the table and headed for the shack and Big Jack.

Chapter Fifteen

The old man had described the layout of the line shack and the best way to approach it without being seen. What Morgan didn't know was that the sheriff had sent a messenger to Nick Baker and Baker had sent one of his men to warn Big Jack.

By the time Morgan got near the shack it was getting dark. He tied his horse to a tree and waited for darkness. He rolled a cigarette and lit it. He smoked the cigarette as he sat on a bank behind some bushes. When he thought it was safe he sneaked up as close as he could to the shack without being seen. He looked around to make sure no one else was near. A lamp was lighted and Morgan walked carefully to the window and looked in. Big Jack was sitting at the table eating supper with another cowboy that Morgan did not recognize. Big Jack had a pistol in his holster and a rifle lying across the table. The other man had a gun in his holster.

Morgan turned toward the front door and tripped over a wooden box.

"There is someone out there, it must be Reeves," bawled a man from behind Morgan.

"That must be him, get him," shouted another man.

Shots came from two different directions, hitting the outside wall of the shack. Morgan cursed himself for being so careless. He turned around and still on his knees started crawling toward the back of the building. He pulled the Navy Colt and held it in his right hand but didn't fire. The bullets were coming closer so he laid down flat on his stomach and waited.

"I can't see him but he was at the window and heading toward the door."

"He must have run because I didn't see him."

Morgan recognized that voice. It was Big Jack. It appeared that they were thinking that he passed by the front. He got back up on his knees and kept crawling as low as he could and reached the back corner of the shack.

"I don't see him here, maybe he went around the back," hollered the one that Morgan didn't recognize.

He didn't have much time to make a decision so Morgan got on his feet and ran as fast as he could toward the woods. "I hear him running toward the woods. Come on let's git him," shouted one of the gunmen.

Morgan knew that he had lost any advantage he might have had so he would have to deal with Big Jack another time. Fortunately, he was nearing the woods. With any luck he could get there and lose what appeared to be four men. He could hear them running after him and firing as they came. A shot whizzed past his right ear just as he tripped and fell hard. He tried to break his fall with his left hand but all that he got was jarring pain in his wrist for his trouble. He tested it to help get to his feet. It was painful but apparently nothing was broken. He was able to get to his feet and made the woods without being hit with a bullet.

He tried to get his bearing as to where his horse was tied. He made his guess and headed toward it, stumbling, bouncing off trees and getting scratched with limbs and briars. He could hear the men cursing and shouting but Morgan was pretty sure that if he could reach his horse he could escape. He would have missed it but suddenly he heard the big roan snorting. He changed directions and quickly reached the horse. He holstered the Navy Colt and swung into the saddle, again the wrist causing him pain but not enough to keep him from mounting.

Morgan could hear the men coming but he knew that they were on foot and he was breaking out into a clearing and the big horse was gaining speed. They would never catch him but he was not happy just getting away. He had not accomplished what he came for.

A couple of hours later Morgan rode into the yard of the Jackson Ranch. In spite of the lateness of the hour a light was on in the house. He dismounted and led the horse into the barn. He found the lantern, lit it, took the saddle off and brushed the horse down. He gave him a generous portion of oats and hay then walked up to the house.

Carla was up and around when Morgan knocked on the door. She came to the door and let him in.

"I'm glad that you are here. I didn't expect you to get back so soon," she said with a smile.

"I didn't expect to be back this soon," he replied as he threw his hat on the table.

"Did you find Jack?"

"Yep, I found him, but he and a couple of his friends found me at the same time."

"I'm glad you survived."

"Thanks, are you sure that you should be on your feet?"

"I think that I'm as stubborn as you are, huh."

"Probably so, anyway I'm heading for the barn to get some sleep."

"Mr. Reeves, you don't need to sleep in the barn, we have plenty of room in the house."

"I better stay in the barn. Good night, I'll see you in the morning."

"Good night," Mr. Reeves.

The next morning Morgan was surprised to find Carla fixing breakfast when he got into the house. Of course with Jamie's help.

"Good morning, Mr. Reeves."

"Good morning, Mrs. Jackson, morning, Jamie."

"Good morning Morgan," replied Jamie with a broad grin on his face.

"You are awful chipper this morning, Jamie. Do you have a girlfriend?"

"Aw shucks, Morgan, you know I'm too young to have a girlfriend," he replied, dropping his head and staring at the floor.

"Come in, sit down at the table before the food gets cold," she admonished the both of them.

When they sat down at the table, Morgan looked across at Carla. "How about you, Mrs. Jackson, are you also too young?"

"Too young for what?" she asked.

"He means to have a boyfriend," replied Jamie.

Carla looked over at Morgan coolly. "Mr. Reeves, I've been looking for lots of things, but not a man. I haven't found even one after Steve that is worth keeping around."

"No offense, Mrs. Jackson, but you are beautiful, smart, a great cook and still young. Your husband has been gone for over two years. Probably not long enough to forget him I reckon but I'm sure that there has to be lots of young men that would be interested in courting you."

"Thank you, Mr. Reeves, I'm flattered. A woman needs those kind words sometimes even if she is not interested in men."

"So then tell me, haven't there been any men coming around after your husband died?"

"As a matter of fact there have been a few I guess."

"I think that you are too modest, Mrs. Jackson. You say just some. Really now?"

"Really, there weren't that many," she said trying to think back to that time. "Of course Nick Baker came around wanting to court me but I let him know quickly that I was not interested in him. He never took the hint and he kept coming back. Finally, he told everyone around town that he would have me or no one would."

"And that scared everyone off."

"There was a man named Billy Walker that came around a few times. Not long afterward he was found ambushed not more than a mile from the ranch here. Of course, like my Steve, no one was prosecuted for the murder. That upset a lot of people but then there was Jimmie Spradlin. He came around a couple times before he was beaten almost to death. He disappeared not long after that and he has not been seen since. After that they just quit coming, except for Baker, of course."

"That's too bad," nodded Morgan.

"Well, like I said, everyone knew that he wanted me and he was rich and powerful. He stole from us and from many other ranches.

He became the most powerful and most ruthless man in the county. I could have been rich and lived like a lady but I just couldn't stand the idea of living with Baker.

"So that's when he shut off credit for you from the bank?"

"Yes, but the best part was that my husband had a statement in our mortgage that the ranch could not be taken over as long as we at least paid the interest on the loan. When Baker and his lawyer came to buy out my mortgage, the banker, who was a friend of ours and a fair man, told Baker he couldn't take it. That made Baker even madder and that's when he cut off all credit for the ranch. I did what I had to do to make sure that the interest was paid.

"But he is still trying," said Morgan.

"Well, he no longer wants to marry me because of my occupation. I'm not good enough to be his lady now, but he still wants the ranch. He has used every means to get me out but I have refused to quit."

"And he has gotten madder and madder at you."

"He sure has and I'm sure that it will get worse since you are here."

"Why do you say that?"

"I was here all by myself and he thought that he was winning. With you here he will have to exert more pressure."

"I'm sure that he is not happy with me being here. I found that out from the folks in town. Would you like more coffee, Mrs. Jackson?"

"I'd like some," said Jamie.

Morgan looked at Carla. "Sure, let him have some. He has worked really hard. He deserves a treat. And yes, I would like some more. You know Mr. Morgan, you are the first man to called me Mrs. since my husband died," said Carla.

"You may be right and I know that you are the first woman to continue to call me Mr. Reeves."

"Well, Mr. Reeves, is there or was there a Mrs. Reeves?"

"Yes, there was one but it was a long time ago."

"Would that have been Brandy that you spoke of in your sleep? What happened to her?"

"That is the one and she died during childbirth," he answered.

"I'm so sorry. I didn't mean to pry."

"Thank you, the memories are still there but it is getting easier to get by."

"I understand what you went through; I'm still going through it with Steve. Is that why you are just drifting?"

"No, not really, I had another problem."

"Do you want to tell me about it?"

"I ... I'm not sure."

"It may help to talk about it."

"Two years ago I was a Marshall in Masonville, Colorado. I had a young deputy and I allowed him to get killed. I ... I don't think that I want to go on with this right now."

"I'm sorry, Mr. Reeves."

"It's not your fault. I think that I need to take care of the horses," he got up and quickly walked out of the house. He sat down on a pile of straw and stared straight ahead. The incident was close to two years ago but sometimes he thought it was just yesterday. Maybe he should talk it out, but with whom? He had not been close to anyone since the incident. Maybe Carla was the one but he couldn't tell her his problems, she already had more problems than she could handle.

Besides, his immediate concern was Big Jack. He lost his chance to get him last night. Well, it was not going to end yet.

Chapter Sixteen

Nick Baker's men found Morgan's trail only a couple of hours after sun up. They followed for an hour or so and Big Jack pulled up his mount.

"Look's like he is heading back to the Jackson Ranch," he said.

"I suspect that by now he has already reached the ranch. What are we going to do now, just ride in and get him?" asked Shorty Hodge.

Big Jack took out a bag of tobacco and some papers, fashioned himself a quirly, took a drag and sat thinking. A half of the cigarette was burned down before Big Jack spoke, "No, we are going back and have a talk with Nick Baker."

He took a few drags before throwing the cigarette down. He turned his horse around, "Come on boys, let's ride."

Big Jack was somewhat concerned about riding in without Morgan's body but Nick Baker could not have been more pleased. Everything was coming together very nicely, even better than he had hoped. Now he could take care of Carla Jackson and Morgan Reeves at the same time. His only question was how best to accomplish the task. He rubbed his sore wrist and every time he did he thought about getting even with that bastard Reeves. When he finally spoke up, he had made up his mind what he wanted to do and how to do it.

"He pulled Big Jack aside and said, "Don't worry about the tracks, I am sure that you are right, he's at the Jackson Ranch. Take all of these men and head for the Jackson Ranch."

"What do you want us to do?"

"Just get as close to the ranch house as you can but stay out of rifle range. Make sure that they know you are there. I want all three of them to worry some, so fire a few shots toward the house."

"What are you going to do?"

"I'm going to town and get the sheriff and while I'm there I'll get Newt Tackett and his friends and town folks. They are already angry and by the time I get finished with them they will be ready to ride to hell and back in order to take care of the whore and his friend."

§

Nick Baker pulled his horse up in front of the Tackett General Store, dismounted and wrapped the reins around the hitching post. He quickly walked up the steps and entered the store. Mrs. Tackett was behind the counter waiting on a customer. Baker interrupted, "Where's Newt?"

She nodded toward the back room, "In the back," she replied with some irritation.

Baker ignored her and entered the back room. "Hello, Newt."

"I heard about that threat my son's killer made toward the sheriff in his own office," said Newt excitedly. "What are we going to do about it?"

"That is not an idle threat, Newt," replied Baker seriously. "Morgan Reeves also made an attempt on Big Jack's life yesterday evening. It was just a clear case of attempted murder."

"Well, what do we do now?"

"We have him cornered at Carla Jackson's ranch."

Newt Tackett's eyes widened, "Do you mean . . ."

"Yes, that's right Newt. That means that she is an accessory after the fact. She's as guilty as he is under the eyes of the law."

"Have you told the sheriff about it yet?"

"No, I thought that you deserved to be told first since it was your son that he killed. Maybe you would want to get your friends together and get out toward the Jackson Ranch. You could be in on the final outcome."

"Yes, you're right. Vengeance, that's what I want."

"You deserve the right to be there. Now I'm going out with my men. I'd suggest that you get your friends together and bring the sheriff with you."

It only took Newt Tackett about thirty minutes to get a crowd of thirty-five armed men formed in front of the sheriff's office. The leader of the group was Newt Tackett with a side arm and a rifle.

The sheriff looked at Newt Tackett and then at the anxious mob. "Tackett, you just said that Baker already has more than a dozen of his own men at the Jackson Ranch. Why in the hell do we need all of these men?"

"All of these folks are here to make sure that my son is going to be avenged," snapped Tackett.

"Hell, Reeves is only one man, why do we need all of these people?" replied the sheriff angrily.

"According to Baker that woman, Carla Jackson, is there also."

"Okay, so there is one man one woman and a child out there against probably fifty armed men."

"Billings, you do your job and lead this posse or the town will find a sheriff that will do the job," growled Tackett.

"This is not going to be a posse; it's going to be a lynch mob," he snapped back.

"What is the difference, Sheriff, as long as we get what we are going out there for?"

"I just don't know about that, Tackett."

"My son was murdered and all of these people are here to make sure that you do your job, so do it and all of these people will be right behind you."

The sheriff was angry but he didn't see any way out of it. "Okay. Okay. I'll lead you but I'm not going to be responsible for anything going wrong."

"We'll be responsible for what happens and what is going to happen is getting rid of a whore and a killer," replied Tackett.

The crowd left town like they were going to a barn dance. Yelling and laughing like they were celebrating Saturday night. Most folks rode horses but some were even driving buggies rented from the livery stable. Whiskey jugs were passed around freely and Tackett urged them on.

What the sheriff had dreaded was about to happen. Revenge, whiskey and a large crowd almost never had a happy ending.

CHAPTER SEVENTEEN

Morgan was in the barn when he heard horses. He couldn't see them but it sounded like ten to twelve. He quickly closed the barn door and ran to the house. "Mrs. Jackson, Jamie, come here quickly," he hollered.

They both came running, "What's the matter?" ask Jamie.

"We got company and it is probably not friendly."

"Who are they?" she asked.

"Not for sure but I'd guess Nick Baker's men."

"What are we going to do?"

"Do you have any weapons and ammunitions in the house?"

"We've got a rifle and a shotgun. Don't know for sure how much ammunition we have."

"Okay. Mrs. Jackson, go get it quickly. Jamie, help me carry those chairs over here toward the doors."

"Okay," replied Jamie, "and I'm not scared."

"Good boy, everything will be okay," replied Morgan even though he was far from certain.

Carla came back with a Winchester 38-40 rifle and a shotgun. She had two boxes of rifle shells and a bag of shotgun shells. The shotgun was a 12 gauge Westley Richards.

"Morgan looked at Carla, "Can you shoot?"

"I usually can hit what I aim at."

"Ma is a good shot, Morgan, I've seen her shoot," said Jamie.

"Jamie, can you load these guns if we need to?"

"Sure, I can do that."

Morgan braced the doors with the chairs and took up a position at one window. It was only a couple of minutes when he heard a voice.

"You in the house, you hear me?"

"I hear you, Jack. What do you want?"

"Oh, I just wanted to make sure that you knew that I was out here with some friends. Listen to this."

A half a dozen shots rang out hitting the outside of the house. "Now what are you going to do?"

Morgan stuck his Henry repeating rifle out of the window and got off four shots. The last one apparently scored a hit because a man screamed. "That's what I'm going to do, Jack."

"That was just a scratch, Reeves. We have plenty of men, guns and ammo and we are going to have a lot more men coming soon."

"What does he mean, more coming?" asked Carla.

"I'd say that the sheriff would be on the way with a posse. Considering how few friends we have, the posse will probably be large and not on our side. Mrs. Jackson, take your rifle and go over to that side window and keep watch and keep your head down, please."

"Mr. Reeves, don't you think that it is time for you to call me Carla? Mrs. Jackson sounds awful formal considering what we have been through in the last few days."

"I guess that would be okay, so long as you call me Morgan."

"Okay, Morgan it is," she replied with a sheepish grin.

"Okay, Carla."

"Morgan, does this mean that you are not going to leave us?" asked Jamie.

"Jamie, we will have to discuss the future later on," replied Carla. Morgan didn't say anything and Carla picked up the Winchester 38-40 and walked over to the other window.

"Can you see anything out of that window?"

"Nothing that looks like a person," she replied.

"Reeves are you still in there?" hollered a deep voice.

"That's Nick Baker, I can recognize that voice anywhere," said Carla.

"Looks like they have gotten their reinforcements. I'm still here Baker. What do you want?"

"I want you to give it up and come out here and bring your whore friend with you," he replied in a loud voice. He roared with laughter and his gunmen joined in.

Morgan, now getting angry, poked the Henry and fired three shots toward the voice. After the smoke settled Morgan hollered out, "Baker, can you guarantee the safety of Mrs. Jackson and the boy if we come out?"

"No deal, Reeves. We are going to tar and feather all of you and probably hang you from a tree until you are dead," he yelled back.

"Baker, is the sheriff out there?"

"He's here what do you want of him?"

"Sheriff Billings, are you out there?"

"I'm here, Reeves, what do you want?"

"You are a lawman. I want you to get the woman and boy out and get them to safety. Then you can do whatever you want with me."

"No, Morgan, I'm not leaving you in here," said Carla.

"Me neither," added Jamie.

"I can't do that, Reeves," replied the sheriff.

"Listen, Reeves, you have no bargaining power. I don't know how you are going to get out of here and you can probably smell that hot tar. That is a horrible way to die," hollered Baker.

"Baker, I'm not asking anything for myself, just let Mrs. Jackson and Jamie go."

"Save your breath, Morgan, I'm not going," Carla replied stubbornly.

"Baker, why can't we let the woman and the boy out? I'm sure we can persuade her to leave the county now," said Sheriff Billings.

"Did you hear that, Newt? The sheriff wants to let these murderers get away," said Baker. "What do you say?

"I say we tar and feather them and if they are not dead hang them from that tree limb over yonder," he replied as he pointed to a large tree some fifty feet away.

"Are you going to tell me that you are going to tar and feather a ten year old boy?" ask the sheriff incredulously.

"Nobody will want that whore's son anyway, we may as well get rid of him with the others," snapped Newt Tackett. "Besides, they killed my boy. Why not do the same to hers?"

"But your son was a grown man and he got himself in trouble," replied Billings.

"Sheriff, you are not going to tell me that you believe that my son was killed in self defense?"

"Tackett, I don't know. I wasn't there but there are some doubts. Dusty said so and he was there."

"Forget it, Sheriff," interrupted Nick Baker. "Dusty is a liar so I fired him. He is probably out of the country by now. Let's get done what we came here to do. Now, Sheriff, do your job."

"If he won't do it give me that badge, I'll get it done," snarled Big Jack.

"Big Jack, you would shoot your grandmother if there was any money in it for you," snapped Billings.

"Why you bastard, I'll tear you apart," yelled Big Jack.

The sheriff pulled his gun, "You step anywhere close to me and I'll blow a whole through that gut of yours and you know that I can't miss at this distance."

Nick Baker stepped between the two. "Hold it both of you. Put that gun down, Sheriff. We have a job to do here, you two can fight later."

"We are wasting time. Let's charge the house and get them out," growled Newt Tackett.

"Tackett, I'm in charge here so just back off. I'll let you know when you can charge the house," said Billings.

"I don't need your permission. Let's move out men," yelled Tackett.

"Just hold on all of you. You can wait at least a short while to get yourself and others killed, can't you?" snarled the sheriff.

"We have some fifty armed men here, those people in the house are the ones going to be dead," replied Tackett.

"Reeves is a gunman and I happen to know that Carla Jackson is an excellent shot with that rifle. What do you think they are going to be doing while you go charging the house?" asked the sheriff.

"So some people may get killed," interjected Baker. "It'll be worth it to get rid of them."

"You mean, so long as it is not you dead and that you get her ranch," said Billings with a sneer.

Baker ignored the sheriff, "Reeves, are you coming out?" he yelled.

"I'll ask you again, Sheriff, are you going to guarantee the safety of Mrs. Jackson and the boy?"

The sheriff hesitated for a moment. The sweat was rolling down his face and into the collar of his shirt. He wished that he was somewhere else, anywhere else.

"Sheriff, you just say no," snapped Tackett.

"I'm sorry, Reeves. I can't guarantee anyone's safety," yelled Billings.

"That doesn't surprise me," replied Morgan. "I guess that you will just have to come in and get us then. Sheriff, do you want the blood on your hands for all of the people that are going to be killed or wounded?"

"I'm sorry, Reeves, I can't help you," replied Billings.

"We are wasting time. I'm going in," yelled Tackett, "Whose coming with me?"

Tackett walked a few steps and a dozen or so men followed him, guns ready. "We're coming in," yelled Tackett.

"There is going to be a lot of dead men out there if you try to come in here," Morgan hollered back.

"As long as you die it won't matter to me," replied Tackett.

Baker looked over at Big Jack, "Hold our men back I don't want them getting mixed up with Tackett's crowd."

"Okay, Boss," replied Big Jack.

"Go ahead, Tackett, see what happens," said Baker.

Tackett wasted no time. He started running toward the house with several men following.

"Don't be a fool, Tackett," hollered the sheriff but either Tackett didn't hear or he ignored the sheriff's warning.

Even though he had encouraged him, Baker was surprised that Tackett agreed to lead the charge.

Big Jack had his men spread out and watch the windows and the front door. "And stay down, we don't want to lose any of you, as least not right away," hollered Big Jack.

When Big Jack was satisfied that the Circle B hands were far off enough not to catch any stray bullets, he returned to where Nick Baker was standing.

Morgan watched them running toward the house and shooting. The bullets were coming close but he waited to return fire. When they were within about fifty feet he open fired. The man immediately next to Tackett's right took a bullet in the gut and went down. The one left of Tackett took a bullet in the knee cap and he also went down screaming with pain. Morgan fired again and hit another man in the shoulder. He staggered a few steps foreword and fell on the grass moaning and groaning.

"Get down," hollered Tackett as he fell and flattened himself on the ground. Fortunately for him, and several others, there was a sink hole that shielded most of them.

"What are you going to do now, Tackett?" asked Morgan.

"We are really going to get you now, you bastard."

"Come on, what are you waiting for?" asked Morgan.

Big Jack looked at Baker, "Tackett is going to get himself and those men killed. The sheriff should be leading that charge."

"Well, either Billings is too smart to lead that group or he is a coward," replied Baker.

"I don't think that Billings is a coward. He and I have had our differences but I'd say that he is being smart."

"Carla, is there any way out of here?" asked Morgan.

"Not that I know of," she replied.

"Morgan, I know how to get out of here," said Jamie.

"Really? Tell me," replied Morgan.

"My dad and I dug a ditch from the back yard and it runs all the way down to the creek. It was supposed to be for watering the garden but right now it doesn't have much water in it."

"That's right, I helped him dig it," added Carla excitedly.

"Is it deep enough to cover us?"

"We'll have to crawl," said Jamie.

"Okay, assuming we can get out of here, is there any place close by to hide out for a few days?"

"There is the rock house up on the hill," said Jamie excitedly.

"Jamie, that is more than two miles and besides it is not a house, it's just walls," corrected Carla.

"Enough to withstand bullets?" asked Morgan.

"Oh, sure it is thick," chimed in Jamie.

Morgan thought for a moment then looked at Carla. Watch this window; I want to take a look. If anyone tries to move in any direction blow their head off."

"Okay, but don't be gone long," she answered.

"I won't," said Morgan as he ran to the back door and opened it carefully. He looked around but didn't see anyone. He got on his knees and crawled out onto the ground. Off to the right was the ditch that Jamie spoke of. He continued on until he could look down in the ditch. It had a couple of inches of water and mud in it but it was deep enough to cover a person on their knees. After looking in all directions to make sure that he had not been seen he turned and quickly crawled back into the house.

"Carla, you and Jamie pack up some food supplies and water we are going to try and get out of here."

"What do we pack?" she asked.

"Anything that is quick to fix or can be eaten without cooking."

"Come on, Jamie, lets pack and get going."

"Reeves, I can't hold all of these people back very long. Are you coming out or not?" hollered the sheriff.

"Sheriff, it looks like we are at a standstill."

"What do you mean?"

"Well, what I want to know is how are you going to get Tackett and his bunch back without me blowing their heads off?"

"Be smart, Reeves, let them go. It will just be a matter of time before this mob gets into the house," replied Billings.

"As I said before, there will be a lot of dead bodies out there before any of you get in. I'll tell you what I will do. I'll let these men go back to where you are without shooting them as a good will gesture."

There was silence for several minutes except for the moaning and groaning from the men hit by bullets coming from Morgan's Henry Rifle. Morgan waited, because he knew that each individual out there had to make up their own mind whether or not Morgan was telling the truth about a truce.

"I got the supplies, all that Jamie and I can carry," said Carla.

"How are we fixed for water?"

"There is a water hole there," said Jamie. "There is plenty of water."

"Okay then just carry a little for the trip. Carla carry my Navy Colt and your rifle, I'll carry the shotgun and my Henry. Jamie you help out."

"Okay," replied Jamie.

"I want you to go and go quickly. I'm going to hold them off as long as I can then I will catch up with you."

"No, no, Morgan don't . . ."

"Carla, please just do as I ask. I don't have time to argue. Now what direction do I go when I get to the creek?"

"Turn west for about a mile an a half then go a few yards north until you find a small trail. Just follow the trail up the hill for a few feet," she answered.

"Good, now go."

She nodded and picked up the supplies then looked at Jamie, "Come on, Son, let's go."

In a matter of seconds they were out the back door. There were no shots so Morgan assumed that everything was all right.

Morgan looked out the window and hollered, "Any of you want to move out or is the truce over?"

"I'm going to trust you but you be damned if you are lying," yelled Ed Bradley. He stood up slowly and walked over to one of the men that was shot. The first one was dead but the second man got up with Bradley's help and they started walking back to the group. Another man jumped up, "Don't shoot, I'm leaving too."

"Go on," shouted Morgan, "I'm not going to shoot right now but I'd suggest you go back to town."

The second man ran over to the man with the shattered knee and half carried him back to the group and out of rifle range. Before they reached the group another man jumped up and ran after them followed by another and finally all of them were abandoning their positions, heading back, including Newt Tackett.

"That is just the beginning, Reeves," hollered Baker. "We have plenty of men left."

"What are you trying to do, get all of them killed?" Morgan hollered back.

"We are going to do whatever we have to do to get you and that woman out of here," replied Baker.

Morgan hollered loud enough for Baker to hear, "Mrs. Jackson, give them a couple of barrels with that shotgun."

Morgan ran over to the window that Carla had vacated, aimed the shotgun and fired one barrel then fired the other. He went back to the other window and hollered out, "Baker, I don't think that Mrs. Jackson likes you very much," yelled out Morgan.

"I don't give a damn about her or you either and no one else out here does either," replied Baker.

Morgan waited a few minutes, "Did you hear me you whore?" hollered Baker.

"Baker, I don't think that she even wants to talk to you," replied Morgan.

Morgan pulled out a bag of Bull Durham and rolled a cigarette. He lit it, took a couple of deep drags and laid the cigarette on the window sill. He wanted Baker to see the smoke and think that they were still in the house. After checking the room to make sure he hadn't left anything, he picked up the last bag of supplies, grabbed the rifle and shotgun and disappeared out the back door.

Chapter Eighteen

Sheriff John Billings was getting angrier by the minute. He was angry that he had all of these folks out here at the ranch and he was angry because Reeves refused to come out. But what he was even angrier about was that Baker and Tackett were trying to usurp his authority. Baker was relatively calm but Tackett was furious because his crusade against Carla Jackson had stalled.

Tackett looked at Baker, "They made a complete fool out of us."

"No, Tackett, they made a fool out of you. You were the one who went off half cocked and got one man killed and two more wounded."

"Just what are you saying?" shouted Tackett angrily.

"I'm saying that you leading those town folks against Reeve's rifle was not the best plan that we could have come up with," he replied calmly.

"You are the one that said I should go," snapped Tackett.

"I thought that you were smarter than to go."

"Well, something had to be done and no one else was doing anything," Tackett snapped sarcastically.

"We'll do something and do it right this time," said Baker with a pause for dramatic effect. "We'll burn them out."

"Hold on, Baker, I'm still the sheriff here, and I can't go along with burning them out. Reeves allowed those folks to get back when he probably could have killed all of them. I think that was a decent thing to do and I think that we should do the same."

"Sheriff, you're loco," said Baker.

"Look, Baker, there are a lot of these men out here that are not too keen on just outright killing them folks the way you want to do," replied Billings.

"Sheriff, I think that you have forgotten your job and your job is what the town folks want done. And don't forget that Reeves killed Newt's son, tried to murder Jack here and without any good reason. And with that woman in there he has killed another man and injured at least two more while resisting arrest. With all of this you want to let by-gones be by-gones?"

"You look here, Baker," began Billings.

But Baker cut him off. "No, you listen to me, Sheriff. You are in this all the way or you are not. If you are not then we will get someone else to wear that badge that will do what he is supposed to do," he shouted savagely.

"You can't fire me, you don't have the authority. Only the town council can do that," retorted Billings.

"We've got close to fifty men and guns here. I think that will give us as much authority as we need," replied Baker.

The sheriff looked at Baker and Tackett then glanced at the crowd that had gathered around the three men. It didn't appear that he was going to get much support. He reached up with his left hand and pulled the badge off his shirt. "I'm not going to be a party to this mob rule so you can do whatever you want to do," replied the sheriff as he pitched the badge to Baker.

"Okay," snapped Baker as he caught the badge and pinned it on Big Jack. "How about you, Jack, can you get the job done?"

"You bet I can," replied Big Jack.

"This is wrong anyway you look at and I'm ashamed to have ever been a part of this mob justice. I can't stop you, so I'm leaving. It doesn't matter who you pin that badge on, it will still be illegal. It will be even more illegal by pinning it on this gun slinging buffoon," said Billings.

Billings saw the big fist coming from the side but he was not able to get out of the way. It connected a glancing blow on his jaw and he would have fallen had he not bumped into another man. He was so angry that he reached for his gun but some one had already taken it out of his holster from behind.

"You have already said enough," said Big Jack. "I'm the sheriff and I'll do what needs to be done."

"That badge will not make you the sheriff and it don't matter how long you wear it," retorted Billings.

"Billings, I'd suggest that you ride and keep riding. There will be no place for you in Twin Creeks after today," said Baker.

"I'll keep your gun, I sort of like the feel and balance," said Big Jack with a sneer. "Besides you won't need it any more."

Without another word John Billings turned, walked to his horse and mounted.

"Hold on, I'm going with you," shouted one of the men. "Me to, said another."

The sheriff turned his horse and rode back toward Twin Creeks with the two men following.

"Okay, Big Jack, you are in charge. Let's get this job done," said Baker with a smile.

"Lets, it has already taken too long," agreed Tackett.

"Okay, Boys, get it done. Josh, get some of the boys together and let's get a fire going then we will burn the place to the ground," said Big Jack.

Josh, one of the town folks, got several people together and started making arrangements for burning the house.

"Look, Baker, I'm with you getting this done but I don't think that this is the way to go about it," said Ed Bradley.

"Get it going, Jack. Bradley you are with us or not, but if you are not then neither you nor your business will any longer be needed in Twin Creeks. Do I make myself clear," growled Baker.

"I just don't like it," he replied.

It doesn't matter whether you like it or not, you just do it," snapped Baker.

CHAPTER NINETEEN

Morgan walked out of the back door, crouched and dashed the few feet to the bank and jumped into the ditch. He splashed when he hit the bottom and quickly got his boots wet and muddy. He ignored the water and mud and started crawling toward the creek.

He wondered how far along Carla and Jamie had gotten. He wished that he could have given them some more time but he didn't think that the mob was going to wait much longer.

Fortunately there were some tall weeds along the ditch so Morgan didn't have to crawl all of the way down to the creek. When he got there he was surprised to see that a hundred yards or so to the right were several horses tied to a rope. They were tied but didn't appear that they were being watched. Obviously they belonged to the mob from town and they were not concerned that anyone would bother them. Instead of going left to follow Carla and Jamie he bent over as low as he could and ran toward the horses. He got there without being spotted and the horses didn't make any noise. He pulled out his hunting knife and walked down the row cutting the reins of all of the horses except for one. He tied the food supplies on the saddle and mounted a big bay horse. He pointed his Henry Rifle straight up in the sky and fired off six shots as he gave an Apache war whoop and started the freed horses down the road toward town.

Once the horses were running he back-tracked and headed toward the rock house and a meeting with Carla and Jamie.

The fire was hot and Big Jack had the men lighting torches to burn the ranch house. "Be careful now, you know that Reeves is a crack shot. I don't want to lose any of you men," said Baker.

"I'm with you, Boss," replied Big Jack.

All of a sudden there came shots and wild bloodcurdling yells from behind the group. "The horses," someone cried out. "They are being stampeded."

"Damn," growled Baker. He had not thought about posting guards with the horses because he didn't think anyone was brave enough or stupid enough to bother them.

"Some of you men get after those horses," hollered Baker.

"Boss, do you think that Billings ran the horses off?" asked Big Jack.

"He may have but I'm guessing that is was Reeves," replied Baker.

"Reeves? He is in the house," interrupted Newt Tackett. "You saw him shooting at us."

Baker stared at the man for a moment. "Newt, have you been in this house?" asked Baker.

Tackett stuttered and said, "Well I . . ."

"I know damn well that you have."

"Why do you ask?"

"Is there a back door in that house?"

"I . . . I never looked for a back door," muttered Tackett.

"I know what you were looking for," he answered scornfully.

"You are mad because you couldn't get in the house with her in it."

"Aw, shut up, Tackett."

He looked at Big Jack. "Jack do we have any men behind the house?"

"Well," stammered Big Jack.

"Get some men back there quickly," ordered Baker.

"Reeves, can you hear me?" hollered Baker.

No one answered and he tried again, "Reeves, answer me."

He stared at the window of the house, "That bastard is gone and took the woman and kid with him," said Baker.

"Now who is the stupid one?" asked Tackett.

"We'll still git 'em. Jack get on with it and get that house burned to the ground," hollered Baker.

"I'm going to lead the charge," cried Tackett.

"They are already gone," said Bradley, "what good would it do us now?"

"It's just the principle of the thing. Burn it down to the ground. We don't want anything left except ashes to remind us about that woman," Tackett answered.

"What happened, did your wife find out that you had been visiting here?" asked Bradley.

"You shut up, Bradley," commanded Tackett.

"I'll say whatever I want," answered Bradley. "I don't like this and even though I'm forced to do it, no one can tell me what to say."

"Both of you help out and stop quarrelling," snapped Baker.

"What do you want us to do about the barn?" asked Big Jack.

"Turn out the animals but don't burn it, I may need that barn when I take over the ranch," replied Baker.

"You are the smart one," replied Big Jack.

Morgan had ridden a half a mile without seeing Carla or Jamie. Luck was holding. He heard a loud boom and he turned to see what it was. Smoke and fire was visible from where he sat on the big bay horse.

"Either they knew that everyone was out of the house or they didn't care," thought Morgan. "Dang, I hope that my roan gets out of the barn."

He would have to worry about him later. He turned back, raked his spurs gently on the sides of the bay and rode on.

CHAPTER TWENTY

Ex-sheriff John Billings was furious as he rode toward town with the two men. He was not that concerned about losing his job as he was the punch that he took from Big Jack. He was still fuming when he heard an explosion. When he turned and looked over his shoulder he saw the smoke from the Jackson Ranch house. "I just hope that they got out before it burned," he thought. "I should have been able to do something."

He was still muttering to himself when they reached Twin Creeks. The two men headed for home and Billings couldn't decide where he was going to go. He thought about going to his room in the hotel to pack his belongings but instead he went directly to the Red Rooster Saloon. He dismounted and walked inside. As he expected, the only person he saw was the mostly drunk bartender Cal Daniels.

"Give me a glass and leave the bottle," ordered Billings.

Even though he was drunk, Daniels could see that Billings was upset and also that he was not packing a side arm. "Lost your pistol?" asked Cal.

"Cal, just give me a drink, I need one bad."

"Okay, Sheriff."

"And don't call me sheriff," he snapped.

"Uh, I don't see a badge. What does that mean?" asked the bartender as he set the glass and bottle on the counter.

"Will you just give me time to wet my whistle? I've had a hard day."

"You ain't the sheriff no more, are you?" he asked.

Billings poured the glass full to the brim with whiskey, picked it up, drained it and set it on the counter. He poured another before he said anything. Then he filled the old man in on what happened during the day and before he finished the old man was laughing loud.

Suddenly he stopped, "Did those folks get out before they set the house ablaze?"

"I don't know for sure but I didn't hear much shooting after I left." He drained the glass and continued, "I know that Reeves would not quit as long as he had ammunition so I assume they got out alive."

"At least for a short while," muttered Daniels.

"I don't know where they would have gone without horses and being chased by a large mob," said Billings thoughtfully.

"You know that boy, Sheriff, he explored all over the ranch. I know that one time he told me about an old prospector's rock house up on the hill. It can't be more than a couple of miles from the ranch house."

"Even two miles is a long way without horses," answered Billings as he poured another glass of whiskey and drained it in one gulp.

"I hope that they made it but it would only be a short time before they would be found anyway."

Billings looked at the old man, "I don't know if I have enough money to pay for this whiskey," said the sheriff beginning to feel the effects of the alcohol.

"Aw shucks, don't worry about it. Baker, Tackett and those other towns folk do-gooders will probably run me out of town anyway if I don't leave first," replied the old man as he took a big swig from the bottle. He pulled out another bottle and set it on the bar. "When you finish with that one you can start on this one," he said.

"I guess that I don't have anything else to be doing now, I might as well drink," the sheriff replied sadly.

CHAPTER TWENTY-ONE

"Have we rounded up the horses yet?" asked Baker.

"Yeah, most of them and we are still trying to round up the rest," answered Big Jack.

"You take some good men and find Morgan's tracks and get after them. Send one of the men back and let me know where they are headed. I'm going to keep Tackett and his men here so that they won't mess up the tracks," said Baker.

Big Jack rubbed the sheriff's badge that he wore crookedly on his chest, "We'll find him, Boss," he replied, assuring Baker that he knew what he was doing.

It was not difficult to figure out what happened. Big Jack and his men went behind the house and found the foot prints and the disturbed ground where the three had slid down into the four foot ditch. They followed the tracks to the creek bank. Footprints went in different directions. Big Jack called back for Boots Magee. Magee was supposedly part Indian and he was an expert tracker having spent several years with General Crook and his army. General Crook, who the Indians called "Nantan Lupan," meaning Grey Wolf was considered the greatest Indian fighter of all.

"What do these signs tells us?" asked Big Jack.

Magee dismounted and walked around in several directions. Only a few minutes later he came back. "From the tracks I'd say that the woman and the boy went to the left and Reeves went right."

"That don't make no sense to me," replied Big Jack. "He was not going to leave them alone after spending all that effort to defend them."

"The only other scenario is that Reeves was the one who stampeded the horses rather than the former sheriff. I did see horse tracks which would mean that he stampeded all of the horses except one and he rode that one," suggested Magee.

"Then that would mean that they split up. Probably the woman and boy left first. If so, they would have a good head start and with Reeves riding a horse he would quickly catch up with them," said Big Jack.

"That's the way I would see it," replied Magee.

"Big Jack, you remember that torn down rock building that belonged to an old miner?" asked Vent Taber.

"I remember it," answered Magee, "and if that is where they went it would be hard to get them out."

"Worth a try, it's only a couple of miles from here," said Taber.

"Can you get us there?" asked Big Jack.

"Sure I can get you there but probably not before those three reach the place," answered Taber.

"We'll take a chance. Shorty, you get back to Baker and explain what we have decided then you come back with the others," commanded Big Jack.

"I'm on my way," replied Shorty as he turned his horse and headed back to the ranch house that was by then mostly ashes.

Big Jack looked at the other nine men, "Let's ride."

Morgan Reeves had ridden about a mile before he caught up with Carla and Jamie. They were wet from sweat and from the water in the ditch and the creek. Their boots and pants legs were muddy from wading through the mud. He dismounted and helped them on the horse. Carla objected but Jamie was so tired he gladly agreed to ride. Carla finally agreed and Morgan stepped out in front of the horse and walked as fast as he could.

After fifteen or twenty minutes Jamie yelled out, "There is the path, see it? It's over there."

Morgan looked at where Jamie was pointing, "Okay, I see it. How far up the hill is it?"

"It's a little ways but it will be difficult for the horse to get here," said Carla.

"You two go ahead and leave the horse when you reach the point where he can't go. I'm going to check our back trail and I'll catch up with you," said Morgan.

"I'm not tired anymore, can I stay with you?" asked Jamie.

"No, I want you to take care of your mother, now git going," answered Morgan.

"Aw shucks," began Jamie.

Carla dug her heels in the horses' side and moved on up the hill without letting Jamie finish his sentence.

Morgan pulled up a small bush and began to try and rub out the tracks that they had made coming in. He was not sure that it would help but he had to do something. He did all that he could with the bush and then hid it behind a small boulder.

He walked several yards on the back trail and climbed upon a boulder. His eyes strained to see if they were being followed yet but no sign. He was sure they would be coming, riding fast but he could not see them yet. He pulled out his Bull Durham and rolled a cigarette. He took several drags before he finally saw riders riding out of some woods about three hundred yards away. He jumped down and ran up the trail as fast as his tired legs would allow him to run.

When he reached a level spot on the hill he looked up ahead and saw that Carla and Jamie had dismounted and tied the horse. They climbed though a narrow crevice only twenty-five or thirty feet ahead. When Morgan reached the horse he checked to make sure all of the supplies and ammunition had been unloaded then led the horse a few yards farther away between two rocks. Hopefully he thought that horse would not alert the others and we would have a few more minutes to get to the place where we hoped to set up a defense. He dropped the reins hoping that the horse would stay put and he followed Carla and Jamie.

"Hurry up, Morgan," hollered Jamie.

Morgan signaled to him to be quiet and the boy turned his head and hurried up behind his mother. Morgan stopped and looked back down the hill but he still could not hear the riders.

Within a few minutes he caught up with the two. "How much farther," he whispered.

Jamie pointed just off to the left and about fifty feet ahead, "Behind that rock."

"Okay, I see it. Let's get there quick," replied Morgan.

It was getting dark and Morgan hoped that the darkness would be to their advantage. It would make more sense to attack during the day time but he was not sure that the leaders of this mob had any sense. Another ten minutes or so went by as the three climbed over the rock and into a foundation that once upon a time was part of a rock house.

"I'm so tired I don't think that I can move another step," said Carla as she dropped the supplies and the guns.

"I'm not tired, what do you want me to do, Morgan?" asked Jamie.

"Where is the water hole?" asked Morgan.

"Over by that wall," answered Jamie.

"Well, how about filling up the canteens, and keep your head down at all times," cautioned Morgan.

"What do you want me to do?" asked Carla.

Morgan looked at the surroundings. On three sides of the house were sheer cliffs that were close to fifty feet and the other was the way they came up. It was steep with a narrow trail that continued on past where they planned to stop. That is the only way that Baker, Tackett and their men could come to get close to them. The good thing was that, at least for awhile, they could hold off the men trying to come through the narrow opening.

"Take your food over on that flat rock and store it with the canteens when Jamie gets back. Make sure that bullets cannot reach them. Getting water when the shooting starts may be difficult, at least during daytime," said Morgan.

"Can we make a fire to cook?" Carla asked.

"I'm afraid not. The flame and smoke will be visible even during the night. We're going to have to eat cold and drink water."

"No coffee?" she asked disappointedly.

"Not tonight.

Jamie came back with the canteens and Carla stored them with the food. "I got some cold biscuits and we haven't eaten for some time," she said.

"I'm game, how about you, Jamie?"

"Me too," Morgan replied.

They ate the biscuits had some beef jerky and washed it down with cold water. Just as they finished Morgan heard voices down the hill. He put his finger to his lips as a sign to be quiet, leaned over the rock and quickly looked down the path where they had come up only a short while ago. He saw nothing. A few minutes later he heard voices and although it was now almost dark he could now see figures down close to where he had left the horse.

"They are here," said Morgan.

"What will they do? When will they attack?" asked Carla.

"I can only make out about a dozen men. I'm sure that they will not attack until the rest of the mob gets here," he answered.

"Don't you think that some of the town's people may have gone home?" she asked hopefully.

"I wouldn't count on that but even if a few men leave there will still be more than forty men down there."

"I don't even think that we have that much ammunition."

"I think that we do but we are not going to be able to miss very often," he replied.

"What do we do now?" asked Jamie.

"Jamie, I want you and your mother to take those two blankets and get some sleep. It is going to be a long night."

"But Morgan, I'm not tired," argued Jamie.

"Come on, Jamie, lets take a nap so that Mr. Reeves can take one later," she said.

"Aw, alright Ma," he answered.

"I thought that we were on first name basis," said Morgan.

"I just forgot," she answered but she was cut off by another voice.

"Reeves, this is the sheriff. We know that you are up there and if you don't come down we are going to come up and get you."

"That would be Jack," said Carla.

Morgan looked at the outline of Carla's face through the dim moonlight. He could tell what she was thinking and it appeared that the decision had already been made. They were going to have to hold off the mob until help came, if any did come.

"Come on down, Reeves, make it easy on yourself."

Even though Morgan knew that the mob was sure that we were up here he did not respond. "Go ahead and try to sleep," he whispered to Carla and Jamie.

They did but about ten minutes later bullets started bouncing off the rocks chipping off chunks and landing close to where Morgan was standing. He moved closer to the big boulder and leaned the Henry Rifle and shotgun against the boulder.

CHAPTER TWENTY-TWO

It was late in the afternoon when two men rode into the small town of Sweetwater. Their horses were worn out and so were the riders. They decided that the first thing that they needed was a drink to pick them up and then later find some food. The first saloon and apparently the only one in town was the Sweetwater Saloon. They dismounted in front, tied their horses and angled toward the place with a crudely painted sign above its doors that read: Sweetwater Saloon. They stepped onto the boardwalk in front of the establishment and pushed through the batwing doors.

The interior of the Sweetwater Saloon was very similar to the saloons and dives that the two men had known all over the west. The air was full of smoke, whiskey fumes and raucous laughter. Several round tables surrounded by chairs were scattered around the narrow, low hung ceiling. In the dim light they noticed that the occupants at three tables were playing poker. At the bar that ran along one wall stood quite a few men drinking beer or downing shots of liquor. A layer of sawdust covered the floor.

One of the two men was close to fifty years old but looked much younger in spite of the increasing gray in his hair. He was about six feet tall and weighed around 180 pounds. He had an angular face with a small scar just under his right eye. His eyes were gray and piercing so that it appeared that he could see through anyone or any thing.

The other man had similar features but was some twenty-five years younger. He was an inch or two taller than the other, had coal black hair and a smile that appeared to be permanently fixed on his face.

"Let's have a drink, find out where to eat and stable the horses," said the older of the two.

"That sounds perfect to me," replied the younger man.

As they headed toward the bar the older man assessed the saloon's customers, judging their occupations by their attire. Most of them appeared to be cowboys wearing range clothes. A few others, dressed in coats and ties, were townsmen or travelers. None of the men seemed to be paying attention to them.

They reached an empty spot at the bar. "What's your pleasure, Gents?" asked the bartender. The bartender was a barrel of a man with a handle bar mustache and thinning hair. He had sleeve garters on his white shirt and wore a blue bow tie.

"Two beers," said the older man. "As cold as you've got."

"Coming right up," he answered while drawing the beers. He slid them down the hardwood bar. "Here you go. That'll be a half-dollar."

The older man was looking through the back bar mirror, and then shouldered his companion, "Red Seiver is at the back table."

"You kidding?" asked the younger man.

"Nope, I'm surprised that I didn't see him earlier. It has been a few years since I seen him but I'd recognize him anywhere."

The younger man turned and stared at the man, "Dad burn it, I believe that you are right. You think that he will recognize us?"

"I'd bet that he would recognize me."

"Let's drink and get out of here," said the younger man.

They drained their beer glasses and the older man dropped some coins on the bar and they turned to leave.

"Well I'll be damn; it is Tom Clay and his boy, Billie. How are things?" asked Seiver.

"Doing fine, Seiver, until we saw you and don't call me a boy," snarled the younger man.

"Well Tom, looks like the boy has grown up to be a young surly wolf," said the man called Seiver.

"I said, don't call me that . . ."

Tom Clay put his hand on his son's shoulder, "Forget it, and let's get out of here."

Two men that had been talking to Red Seiver at the table stood and blocked the path toward the front door. "Going somewhere, Gents?" asked one of the men.

"Now, Hobie, you know that these men would not leave without having a drink with us," said Red with a sneer.

"Look Red, we have been riding all day and we are tired and hungry so we don't feel like having a drink with you tonight," answered Tom.

"You see, Red, he thinks they are too good to drink with us," shot back Hobie Sharp.

"Okay, Hobie you can put it any way that you want but we are not having a drink with you so I'd suggest that you get the hell out of our way."

"I guess that you will just have to move those boys, Tom, because I don't think that they are going to move even if you say please," replied Red sarcastically.

"If that's what it takes," replied Billy. "Then we might as well get it done."

"Big talk, Boy," said Red, "what do you think, Bobbie Jack?"

"I think that it will be as easy as strolling through the rose garden," he answered with a snicker.

"Pop, what are we waiting on, how long are we going to take this abuse?" asked Billy.

"Bill, I would prefer to avoid a fight if possible," his father replied. "Siever, we have no quarrel with you or men."

"Well, guess what, you are not going to be able to avoid a fight," said Hobie.

"Tom, it looks like you got your answer," replied Seiver.

"I guess we did," said Tom as he lifted his left arm slightly. Billy nodded briefly in understanding.

"Red, it's your call you get to go first," snapped Tom.

"I don't mind being first as long as I stand up last," said Red with a loud laugh, as he reached for the gun at his hip.

His gun cleared leather but he rocked back with a bullet in the chest from Tom Clay's .45. He collapsed in a heap and was dead before he hit the floor.

Tom's second shot tore through the throat of Hobie Short and he also died on the way to the floor, Billie Clay's first two shots hit Bobby Jack, and one hit him in the belly and the second in the chest.

Tom Clay looked around the saloon, "Anyone else joining in?"

There was muttering among themselves but no one chose to join in. "Good, I need another beer, how about you, Billie?"

"Dobson, go get the marshal and the undertaker so that we can get these bodies out of here."

The old man named Dobson shuffled out of the saloon and walked down the sidewalk toward the marshal's office.

"I was just thinking the same thing about the beer, Pop."

"Two beers, Barkeep," said Tom.

"It'll be a pleasure gents and it'll be on the house," replied the bartender.

The bartender placed two full glasses on the bar, "My name is Mike, and everyone calls me Big Mike."

Billy Clay looked the bartender up and down, "I can see why they call you Big Mike," said Billy with a smile.

"You can't miss this body," said Big Mike with a loud laugh.

"By the way, Big Mike, where would two hungry cowboys find a good steak?" asked Billy.

"That would be Rosy's Café and her steaks are great."

"Drink up, Billy, and lets go find Rosy," said Tom as he drained his glass.

He looked back at Big Mike, "Thanks for the drink and tell the sheriff we will be at Rosy's Café if he needs us."

"Be glad to, Gents."

The two men left the saloon, untied their horses and walked toward the livery stable a block away. An old gray haired man greeted them at the door, "Evening, Gents, you staying the night?"

"Yes, and we have been riding hard so I want you to take good care of these animals," said Tom.

"I'll do it, will cost you half a dollar apiece."

"Sounds reasonable," replied Tom as he handed the coins to the old man.

The two men walked quickly to Rosy's Café and took a seat in the back so that they could watch the front door. There were only two other tables with people at them. A middle aged woman walked up to the table, "My name is Rosy, what'll you boys have?"

"Hello, Rosy, I'll have steak, eggs, potatoes and biscuits with a pot of hot coffee," answered Tom.

"Me too, Rosy, and make my steak rare," added Billy.

"Thanks, Boys, and I'll get your orders out right away," she said as she smiled and walked away.

Before they knew it she came back with a pot of coffee and two cups. She poured coffee into the cups and left the pot before heading back to the kitchen.

They had only drunk half of the first cup when the marshal walked in. He looked around the room, spotted the two and headed toward their table.

"Hello, Boys, names George Benson and I'm the marshal of this here town."

"Glad to make your acquaintance, Marshal. My name's Tom Clay. This here is my son, Billy."

"Glad to meet you both," replied the marshal.

"Have a seat, Marshal, and have some coffee," offered Tom.

"Don't mind if I do."

Rosy came back to the table with a cup and filled it from the pot on the table. "Evening, George, want something to eat?"

"No thanks, Rosy, I'll just have coffee."

Rosy looked at the two men, "Your food will be out in a moment, Boys."

"Thank you, Ma'am, we are much obliged," answered Tom.

"You have any issues with the shooting?" asked Tom.

"No, I'm aware of your reputation as a lawman, Tom, so I don't have any problems. I guess that I'm a little curious about why you are in Sweetwater."

"I'm curious as to how you knew that we were lawmen?" asked Billy.

"Well, young man, the way that you walk and talk and besides those two rusty holes in your father's white shirt is a dead give away.

Nothing other than a lawman's badge would leave those holes," he replied with a smile.

"You must have good eyes, Marshal, most people would not have seen that," answered Billy.

"It's not necessarily good eyes, it's trained eyes. That is what I hope will allow me to outlive all of the outlaws that I meet."

"You have to be aware of everything," said Tom Clay. "Anyway, I don't mind telling you, Marshal, we are heading to Twin Creeks. We understand that a friend of ours is in trouble."

"That would be Morgan Reeves," said the sheriff.

"Yes, but how do you know him?" asked Billy.

"I've never actually met him. I understand that he was here a few days ago to see me but I was out of town."

"Sure, he sent us a telegram from here," said Billy.

"What do you know about the situation over there?" asked Tom.

"I'd say that your friend is in deep trouble. I know Sheriff John Billings over there and he was a good lawman once but he is in over his head with the ranchers, like Nick Baker and other townsfolk."

Rosy came back with the food and the two men ate hungrily. When he was nearly finished Tom looked at the marshal. "How far is it from here to Twin Creeks?"

"A good eight hours if you have good and rested horses," replied the sheriff.

"We have very good horses but we have been riding for three days. I can't say that they are rested."

"I wish that I could help you out with horses but I really don't have any to spare."

"Well thanks anyway, Marshal, but I think we would prefer to ride our own. What do you know about Baker?" asked Tom.

"He's rich and powerful and his money came from questionable sources. Unfortunately, there is not enough evidence to prosecute."

"Thanks for the information, Marshal," said Tom.

"Glad to do it, good luck to you both."

"Thanks, Marshal. Billy, you ready to find a room?"

"I sure am. I probably could sleep for a week."

"How about until seven in the morning?" replied Tom.

Billy laughed and followed his father to the door.

"The Sweetwater Hotel is the only one in town but it is clean and the prices are reasonable. Just tell Nate that I sent you and he will fix you right up," said the sheriff.

"Thanks again, Marshal."

Tom and Billy left the café and a few minutes later Marshal Benson stood and left the café, heading to his office.

The two men found the Sweetwater Hotel, rented two rooms and a short time later they were sound asleep.

CHAPTER TWENTY-THREE

Big Jack and the men continued to trail Reeves until they located the path up the hill that Vent Taber had described. They stopped and dismounted while Taber surveyed the area. He came back shortly, "That is the place but like I said earlier, it's going to be tough getting them out. It's solid rock."

Big Jack had hollered up to Reeves but he got no answer.

"Look, Big Jack, I've been on this ranch for a long time and I've put up with and participated in Baker's criminal acts but this is not right," said Pete Cordell.

"Spit it out, Pete, what are you saying?" asked Big Jack.

"I'm saying that there comes a time when a man has to stomp his own snakes. These snakes belong to Nick Baker and Newt Tackett, so why are we stomping them and maybe getting ourselves killed in the process. And just for them and the small amount of money that Baker pays us," he replied.

"Because we are riding for the brand and that small amount that you are talking about is good money around here. I would not suggest that you talk like that in front of Baker," he snapped.

"Well maybe someone needs to tell him," replied Pete as he walked away.

At that point Baker and Tackett came riding up with the group of townsfolk. The two men dismounted and walked toward Big Jack.

We have got them spotted but it is awful dark to try and move in with all of the cover that they have," said Big Jack.

"Where are they?" asked Newt Tackett.

Big Jack described in detail the location of the three people then he looked at Baker. "Unfortunately, we only have one way through those rocks and it is a very narrow crevice."

"Have you seen any of them?" asked Baker.

"No but we know they are up there," replied Big Jack.

"We found the horse that they rode. He is over there behind that clump of bushes."

"Okay, we'll have plenty of time to smoke them out. Let's get some coffee going. Newt, send some men to town and get some supplies. We need to feed this group, we don't want any of them to decide that they have to leave here to eat," said Baker.

"Wait a moment, Baker, you want me to feed all of these people?" Who is going to pay for it? questioned Tackett.

"Don't forget that it is your son that we are avenging," replied Baker.

"I'm not forgetting and I'm also not forgetting that you are the one that wants that woman's land," Tackett snapped back.

"Okay, we'll split the charges, now get going so that we can get this job over and finished," said Baker.

Tackett mumbled as he turned and walked back to where the crowd was waiting. He assigned a couple of men to make the trip and gave them instructions as to what they were to bring back with them. They left for town and Tackett came back to where Big Jack and Nick Baker were discussing strategy.

"We are going to continuously fire in the direction where they are, we may not be able to hit any of them but we don't want them to get comfortable or be able to sleep," said Baker.

"I'll get some men and spread them out as far as we can and I'll have them shoot every twenty or thirty minutes," replied Big Jack.

"That would be great; however we need some rifles with special sights for sharpshooters. Once it gets daylight we may be able to get close enough to hit them," commanded Baker.

Big Jack turned away but Baker stopped him "Talk to Newly and have him get to town and get some repeating rifles from his store and bring them back. And tell him to outfit them with sights," said Baker.

"What if he does not want to furnish his own guns?" asked Big Jack.

"Tell him if he wants to do business with the Baker ranch he'll do what he is told," snapped Baker.

When he heard the request, Newly Thompson was glad to provide the guns. He hoped that this would give him a leg up with Nick Baker against the other gunsmith. Baker could steer a lot of work to him if he wanted. As soon as Big Jack told him what they wanted he mounted his horse and headed for town.

Morgan looked down the hill where some forty armed men were congregated close to a fire. "It looks like some people are having coffee tonight."

"It is getting colder up here, it would be nice to have something warm to eat or drink," answered Carla. Just as she finished speaking, bullets began hitting all around where they were sitting.

"Stay down both of you," said Morgan.

"Do they really expect to hit us from down there in the dark?" Carla asked.

"I doubt it. I suspect that they want us to be edgy and as uncomfortable as possible during the night," Morgan replied.

"Why would they want to do that?" asked Jamie.

"Jamie, people that are nervous, get no sleep and on edge are more likely to make mistakes," replied Morgan.

"I think I understand," he replied. "And I'm getting cold."

"Just get the blanket and roll yourself up in it. That's all that I can think of," responded Carla.

A few minutes later the bullets started again. "Two can play this game," said Morgan as he took his Henry repeating rifle and fired six times toward the fire flashes from the group.

"You are wasting ammunition," hollered Baker.

"Oh, we have plenty enough," hollered back Morgan.

"We have just sent someone to get more so that we can keep you awake all night and maybe even hit one of you," replied Baker.

"Where is the sheriff, isn't he supposed to be in charge of the posse or should I say mob?" answered Morgan.

"I'm the new sheriff," replied Big Jack. "Aren't you going to congratulate me Reeves? How about you, Mrs. Jackson, are you going to congratulate me?"

They both ignored Big Jack. "What do you think happened to Sheriff Billings?" asked Carla.

"I don't know but obviously he is no longer in charge of this group. That is not good for us. He may not like either of us but he is more likely to try and control the crowd," replied Morgan.

"You have nothing to say?" hollered Big Jack.

Morgan took the Henry and fired three quick shots in the direction of the voice. "That is my answer."

Almost thirty minutes passed before the firing started up again, Morgan ignored the shots.

Jamie stirred but went back to sleep. "Are we going to be able to get out of here alive?" asked Carla.

"I wish I could answer that question but all I know is that we are going to fight. If we go we are going to take a lot of people with us."

"Morgan?"

"Yes."

"I want to say something just in case we don't get out of here. I really didn't mean to pry in your past, can you forgive me please?"

"We are going to get out somehow and there is nothing to forgive, Carla. I shouldn't have reacted the way I did."

"I know that we might not get out of here alive so I just don't want to go without telling you how much I appreciate you and what you have done for me and Jamie."

"I'm going to do everything that I can to make sure that we do get out, but anyway I want to explain what happened."

"You don't have to. I shouldn't have asked."

"I want to," he interrupted.

"It began a little more than three years ago when I was a deputy marshal in Masonville. A man named Tom Clay was the marshal. We worked very well together and also became good friends. Some time later Tom decided that he wanted to run for the county sheriff's job and he recommended me as the town marshal. Tom was quite popular so he won the election and became the sheriff.

The Masonville town council followed Tom's advice and named me the town marshal."

"Tom had two sons. The oldest is named Billy and the youngest was named Tom Junior after his father. Billy was also a deputy marshal in Masonville but when the old man became county sheriff, Billy left with him and became a deputy sheriff. Young Tom was only twenty years old and he had been working in a law office and studying law in Denver. I was not sure exactly why young Tom came home but it was rumored that it had something to do with a girl that he was seeing. Carla, I know that this is a long and boring story. Are you sure that you want me to continue?"

Carla reached over and put her hand on his and spoke softly. "Morgan you haven't spoken that many words at one time to me since I have known you. I want to hear it and maybe you may need to tell it to someone."

"You are a wonderful and understanding woman, Mrs. Jackson."

She kept her hand on his. "I don't know very many people that would agree with you, especially since most that I know are trying to kill me," she laughed nervously.

"They haven't done it yet. All we can do is play out the hand that we have been dealt."

"I trust you and whatever happens I can accept it."

"I don't know that trusting me is a smart move but anyway, Little Tom was fascinated with lawmen, probably because of his father and brother. So, he wanted to become a deputy sheriff like his older brother Billy but Old Tom said no. He wanted Little Tom to go back to Denver and continue studying law. Young Tom approached me about becoming a deputy marshal and him working with me. At first I said no, but he continued to come around and ask for a job. I needed a deputy so finally I approached the sheriff about hiring the young man as my deputy. At first he said no but after talking to his son he told me that he didn't think that young Tom was going back to Denver so against my better judgment I hired the boy."

"Young Tom was a bright young man and growing up with his father and brother being lawmen he learned how to handle himself. He also became good with a gun. He had only been working for about three months when five men came into town and robbed the express office. They took ten thousand dollars and got away clean. Several hours later when I got back to town I got a posse together to go after them. I requested that young Tom stay in town and take care of things while we were gone. He was stubborn just like his father, so he insisted that he ride with me and the posse. So I left my other deputy Sid in town. Sid was older and more experienced so I should have taken him with me."

He paused for a moment and built a smoke. He bent down behind a rock in order to hide the flame from the match. Then he lit the cigarette and took a deep drag, inhaled and let the smoke come out slowly.

Carla listened intently and waited for him to begin again.

Morgan hesitated for a moment, rolling over the events in his mind before trying to go on. He was thinking how to tell the story that would hurt him less emotionally. "The posse consisted of me, young Tom and five other men. The tracks were fairly easy to follow so we made good time. We camped out over night and began again the next morning. We had been riding about four hours on the second day when we caught up with them. They were hiding out in an abandoned cabin. Some of the posse members recognized their horses so we were sure that we were on the right track."

Morgan took the last drag on his cigarette and crushed it out under his heel. "Let me get you a drink of water," said Carla as she crawled over a few feet and found the canteens.

She crawled back and handed one to him. He unscrewed the lid, took a short swallow and closed it back up. "It is probably time for the shooting so I'll wait before finishing the story," he said.

It had not been more than a couple minutes when the shooting began again. Morgan figured that they had spent nearly thirty rounds before they stopped.

"Are you still up there Reeves?" hollered Big Jack.

Morgan ignored the illegal sheriff and waited to see what would happen next. He crawled a few feet where he had a better view of the cut out. He knew that this would be the easiest way for the men to attack and he was wondering why they hadn't already tried to come through. He could see the rocks because of the camp fire but did not have a low view if the men were crawling through the cut. He couldn't hear anything either and he figured that they were safe, at least for the time being.

He crawled back to where Carla was setting. "Jamie woke up but he went back to sleep with his head in my lap," said Carla quietly.

"It has to be rough on the little feller," replied Morgan. "He is a good boy."

"I'm glad he really likes you too. By the way, I'm not very little but it is rough on me also. No coffee, no cooked food and having to crawl around in the dark on rocks have to be rough on everyone. My knees and elbows are raw and bleeding," she said sadly.

"I'm sorry, Carla."

"I don't mean to whine. Please go on with the story."

"Well we had them pinned down but they would not come out and it was going to be difficult for us to get in without losing some men. One of the men had been in the cabin a few years ago and he thought that there was a small window in the back. He thought that it was high up so it would be difficult to get in but it might be worth a try. I asked the man to move carefully to the back and make sure that there was a window and try and see if anyone was guarding the window. He was gone for several minutes and when he got back he reported that in fact there was a window but it was small and high off the ground. He reported that he could not be sure but he didn't think that it was guarded."

"While we discussed the situation the man said that he and three other men in the posse were too big to try and get through the window. The other man, Curt, had been crippled when thrown from a horse some time back and he didn't move around good enough to get through the window. That left me and young Tom. I had already decided that I was the likely choice to make the move but young Tom insisted that since he was younger and quicker that he should be the one to try it. The other thing that convinced me was that I was the best shot of the group in case we had a shoot out. I knew then that I was making a mistake but I allowed young Tom to try and get through the window."

Morgan hesitated again and rolled another cigarette. He lit it and took a couple of drags.

"We cut loose at the front of the cabin in order to keep their attention and allow young Tom to get to the window without being seen. He was supposed to wait to get inside until he got the signal from me. We were to stop firing, wait a minute as the signal to him that we were moving closer and start firing. We stopped firing when we saw him get behind the cabin but before we fired the three shots to let him know we were moving closer we heard shots from the back of the cabin. I knew that it was bad for him but we didn't know for sure for another three hours when we finally killed two of them and two more surrendered. When we got in the cabin the fifth man was dead and young Tom was dying. All that he would say was that he was sorry that he let me down."

"I'm really sorry, Morgan. His father didn't blame you, did he?" asked Carla.

He crushed his cigarette and waited for a minute before they started and stopped shooting again. "No, he didn't blame me and that made me feel even worse. We carried the body back to town and I went to talk to the old man."

After I explained the events surrounding young Tom's death his father just shook his head and said, "I'm glad that his mother was not around to witness his death," then he left walking toward the undertaker.

"I just didn't know what to say or do," said Morgan.

"How did Billy take it?" asked Carla.

"He took it really hard but he tried to assure me that it was not my fault and that it was just something that happened when wearing a badge. He never blamed me for it."

"And his father, did he get over it?" she asked.

"He talked to me later and he also tried to tell me that it was not my fault."

"But you knew better, didn't you?"

"Yes I did. If I had gone to the window myself the boy would still be alive."

"Morgan, I've been around a while and I know lots of lawmen. They always tell you that they are taking a risk when they pin on a badge. Young Tom wanted to pin on a badge. If you didn't give him a chance someone else probably would."

"Probably, but we don't know that for sure," he argued.

"What we do know is that when a man wants something badly enough then he usually finds a way to do it. That is exactly what young Tom did," she replied.

"You know, that is exactly what Tom Clay told me as I was leaving town."

"You didn't stay around for the funeral?" she asked.

"I stayed until after the funeral and a couple days longer. I couldn't get the incident out of my head so I decided to move on."

"And how long have you been riding?"

"It has been close to two years now. I resigned as marshal and I had a meeting with the sheriff before leaving. He tried hard to get me to change my mind but I just couldn't stand to walk the streets and go to the places where young Tom had hung out. I packed my few meager belongings and rode out. I rode aimlessly, not caring where so long as the trail took me away from the town and the nightmarish memory of that boy."

"Did you ride far enough to outrun the memories?" she asked quizzically.

"No, the memories went as fast as I did. I've decided finally that I will never forget and that I'll have to live with it."

"I'm really sorry. I wish that I could say something that would help, but I can't."

"Thanks for listening anyway."

"You have not talked to Tom or Billy since?"

"No I have had no contact until a few days ago when I telegraphed Tom from Sweetwater."

"When was that?" she asked puzzled.

"It was when I rode over to Sweetwater to get supplies. I tried to contact the sheriff over there but he was out of town."

"Did you ask for help?" she asked.

"I put in the telegram what we were facing but I don't know that he will even get the message and if he did, would he even come this far."

"So you didn't want to tell me, in case he didn't come?"

That's about the size of it."

"So we still have a chance," replied Carla.

"A chance but it is probably only a slim chance. Now I think that you need to get some sleep, you may need to spell me after a while," he said.

"I'll get a short nap. Wake me up in an hour and I will watch while you sleep," she replied.

CHAPTER TWENTY-FOUR

Cal Daniels and the ex-sheriff, John Billings, had been drinking for several hours. It was Daniels stated goal to drink all of the whiskey in the bar before he left town for good. They had drunk so much that he and the sheriff were close to being out on their feet. Neither knew what time it was but they heard a buggy roll into town and some male conversations.

Billings, carrying his bottle, stumbled to the swinging doors of the saloon, pushed them open and looked out. He looked back over his shoulder. "They stopped in front of Tackett's general store," he announced.

"Aw, Sheriff you are so drunk you probably cannot see anything that far," replied Daniels.

"I've got good eyes, they may be a little blurry but I can still see fine."

"Okay then why would anyone be at the store during this time of the night?"

"You old sop, you don't even know what time it is."

"I'm sure that you don't either but I do know that it is dark."

"How do you know? You haven't been outside in hours"

"I feel it in my bones," Daniels chuckled.

"At this time I don't think that you can feel anything with all of that rot gut whiskey you have been drinking. Some one is coming this way."

"I better hide the whiskey," stammered the old man.

"Why would you want to do that, this is a saloon?"

"Oh, for a moment I forgot where I was."

Vernon Wells came in through the door. "I need several bottles of whiskey."

"I think that we drank all of it," replied Daniels.

"We have plenty," said the ex-sheriff, "the question is do you have any money?"

"It is for Baker, Tackett and the rest of the men," snapped Wells.

"Then I think that Baker and Tackett should come in and pay for it," replied Daniels.

"Okay, I don't have time to argue with you, you old drunk."

"You are not arguing with an old drunk, you are arguing with me," chuckled Daniels.

Wells looked at the old man, pulled some money from his pocket and dropped it onto the bar. "Give me five bottles."

Daniels picked up the money and put five bottles of whiskey on the bar. "There you go, Slick."

"My name is not Slick, aw never mind," he turned to go but Billings stopped him.

"What's going on out there?"

"We have Reeves, his woman and the boy trapped up on the hill by the old rock house. We are going to flush them out when it gets daylight."

"That might not be easy to flush them out, that is a fortress up there and Reeves is a pretty good shot with that rifle and a six gun."

"We still have nearly forty men out there. I don't think that they can last very long once we start shooting."

"What are you loading from the store?" asked Billings.

"Mostly food supplies, Baker wants to feed everyone in hopes that they will not leave."

"I bet that old skin flint Tackett is raising cane if he is going to give away all of this stuff," said Daniels.

"He isn't they had a big argument and Baker decided to help foot the bill. Well I gotta git going, see you later."

"What do you think their chances are of getting out alive?" asked Daniels when the man left the saloon.

"I'd say pretty slim for the long term."

"Oh well, lets finish drinking this whiskey," suggested Daniels.

"I think that I have had enough."

"What are you going to do then? Are you going to the hotel?"

"No, I'm going to sit in this chair and sleep enough so that I can get up from here and go to the hotel so that I could go to bed. I don't know how long that will take but I got nothing else to do anyway."

"That makes some sense to me, I guess," replied Daniels.

A couple of hours later the ex-sheriff was awakened by the gunsmith, Newly Thompson. He also had come into the saloon for some whiskey. However, it was not for anyone else, it was just for himself.

"What are you doing back here in town, Newly?" asked Billings.

"Well, Baker wants me to get some guns and fix them with special sights so that they can roust out those folks in that rock house. And I need a couple of bottles of whiskey to keep me warm."

"Newly, there are only three people in there and one is a woman and another is a ten year old boy. Why in the hell does he need more guns?" asked Billings.

"They don't need more guns they need special sights on repeating rifles. Say, Sheriff, you have several repeating rifles at your office. How about you letting me borrow some of your guns from the jail?"

"Now why would I want to do that?"

"Because Baker wants guns and I'm short right now."

"You are the gunsmith, how can you be short on guns?" asked Billings.

"I had to sell some to the town folks before they headed out with Baker. Come on, Sheriff, I'll get them back to you."

"Look, Newly, I'm not the sheriff anymore and you already know that. Also I'm not going to give you guns that belong to the town so that you idiots can murder a woman and a child."

"Alright, I guess that I'll just have to take what I have at the store. I'll see you, Sheriff; oh excuse me, Mr. Billings."

"Newly, take some good advice and don't take anymore guns up there. This whole thing could blow up in your face. The federal government may send in marshals and arrest everyone involved," suggested Billings.

"What do you mean? It is a legal posse, isn't it?"

"Look, Newly, the fact that Baker pinned a badge on Big Jack Coleman does not make any of this legal. He had no authority to get rid of the sheriff or appoint another one," he explained.

"But if I do this job for Baker, he may decide to do more business with me and I need the money. Can I get the whiskey now?"

"Get yourself the bottles and leave the money on the counter. So this is all about money, and you are not concerned about going to jail or getting yourself killed."

"No, but..."

"But nothing, Baker may be dead or in jail and you may be with him."

"I'll think about it," he replied as he left the saloon with a bottle of whiskey in each hand.

CHAPTER TWENTY-FIVE

Morgan allowed Carla to sleep and she didn't wake until just before daylight. She fussed at him for not awakening her earlier but he figured that she needed the sleep more than he did. Jamie was also wide awake and trying to remember what happened last night.

Morgan decided to go ahead and make coffee to try and get rid of the chill in his bones. He hid the fire as much as he could. Even though Baker and his men knew that they were up in the rocks he didn't want to leave anything that they could specifically aim at.

The fire was small but hot and soon he had the coffee boiling. He also cut off some bacon strips and put them in an iron skillet. In a few minutes the bacon was sizzling. Jamie was excited since he had not had a hot meal for several hours.

"Can I have some coffee when it is done?" he asked.

"Certainly, Jamie, I'm going to give you the first cup when it is finished. Uh, that is if it is okay with your mother."

"Ma, please?"

"That is okay with me, as long as I get some also."

"You can have the second cup, Mrs. Jackson."

"Morgan pulled out a tin cup and poured a half cup and handed it to Jamie. "Drink up big man."

He poured another cup for Carla and then poured himself one. Even though the coffee was really hot Morgan drank about half of his cup without stopping. He felt the burning sensation going down his throat but he began to thaw out from the chill that had struck him over night.

He then went over and dished out two plates of bacon and some left over biscuits and gave them to Jamie and Carla. When he was finished he dished out some for himself and sat down next to where they were sitting.

Carla finished her food and looked at Morgan. "What do you think that they will do now?"

"I would say that once they are ready they will rush us once to find out how well we are defended. If that doesn't work quickly, I suspect that they will take their time and lay siege against our location."

"Can they get through that narrow passage?" asked Jamie.

"Yes they can but it will be difficult during the daylight because it is so narrow that only a couple of people can get through it at a time and we can see them. I guess that I'm surprised that they didn't try to sneak through while it was dark," he replied.

Carla pushed a wisp of hair from her eyes and asked, "So what is the plan?"

Morgan gazed at her for a moment and thought about how beautiful she was. "Well, you and I are going to keep a watch at the passage and try and keep them out. Jamie I need for you to reload the guns for your mother and me. Can you do that?"

"Oh, sure I can do that," Jamie replied excitedly.

"Then I need you to lay out the bullets for each gun separately and when they are empty you reload them."

Jamie went to work laying out the shells on a flat rock. "Carla, you need to use the 38-40 and shoot after I stop shooting. With that we will have a constant barrage going into the passage way."

"We only have six shotgun shells," announced Jamie.

"Okay, I'll hold the shotgun until they get really close. Hopefully they won't get that close."

"I'm glad that you are going to fire that thing. It hurts my shoulder something fierce," said Carla.

"I know it knocked me down when my dad let me fire it once," said Jamie.

"Did you ask him to let you fire it again?" asked Morgan.

"Shucks no. I could feel the pain in my shoulder for several days after that. I let Pa do the shooting with the shotgun after that."

Just then the shooting from below began. It lasted for several minutes but Morgan and Carla held their fire.

"Get ready Carla they'll probably be coming any time now."

"I'm ready as I'm ever going to be," she answered.

CHAPTER TWENTY-SIX

Before daylight Tom and Billy Clay awoke, dressed and walked to the livery stable. They quickly saddled their horses and walked them out of the barn and down to Rosy's Café. They walked in and looked around. The only customer in the place was Marshal Benson. Tom headed toward the marshal's table and Billy followed.

"Morning, Boys," said Marshal Benson cheerfully.

"Morning, Marshal, I hope that you had a restful night," replied Tom.

"I did, I slept well. You boys sit down and have some coffee and some grub before you ride out."

"Thanks, Marshal, I'd be glad to," replied Billy.

"Me too," said Tom.

A middle aged woman came to the table with two cups and poured coffee from the pot on the table. "Are you gents planning to eat?"

"Sure, steak, eggs, and potatoes with biscuits," said Billy.

"And you, Mister?"

"I'll have the same. Scramble the eggs and burn the steak," he answered.

"You got it. Help yourself to more coffee," she replied as she headed back to the kitchen.

"How long did you say it will take to get to the city of Twin Creeks?" asked Tom.

"I'd say six to eight hours if you are lucky. There is some rough terrain on the way so you'd best be careful. You lose a horse and it'll take you twice as long," warned the sheriff.

"We'll be as careful as possible but we need to get there as quickly as we can."

"About ten miles out there is a cutoff that will save you some time but it is rougher than the other. It could save you an hour or so."

"We'll decide when we get there," replied Tom.

"When you reach the fork on the other side you will only have an hour and half or so," said the sheriff.

"I like that part," offered Billy.

The waitress came back with the food and the two men ate as quickly as possible and then left coins on the table to pay for the meal. They spoke to the marshal and left the café. They mounted and rode out at a rapid pace.

§

Baker, Big Jack, and Newt Tackett were in a serious conversation. "Jack it is time for us to get this job finished," said Nick Baker.

"I'll lead the charge," said Newt Tackett.

"Yes, like you did before and almost got yourself killed," laughed Big Jack.

"Big Jack, I haven't seen anything that you have accomplished so far except for allowing those people to escape. If you had done what you were supposed to do they all would be part of the ashes back where the house used to be," snapped Tackett angrily.

"Why you pip-squeak, I'll tear you apart," hollered Big Jack.

"Jack, you are nothing but a bully. You pick fights only with people that you can whip. And that is why you didn't save my son's life. You were afraid of Morgan Reeves and still are," Tackett hollered back.

Big Jack whipped out his .45 and aimed it at Tackett. Baker slapped it down. "I've got more important things to do than watch you two kill each other."

"Baker you had better keep this old man away from me or he won't last very long," snarled Big Jack.

Ed Bradley was standing close and within ear shot chimed in, "Baker you see what you are allowing to happen now. We are fighting each other and we have no idea how many of us will get through this alive."

"Bradley, your job is to follow orders. Big Jack here is the sheriff and it's his job to make sure that this job is finished," growled Baker. "What would you have us do, just walk away?"

"I'd just like to hear the other feller's side before I kill him," Bradley snapped back.

Big Jack's hand fell over the butt of his gun.

"Bradley, do you want us to walk away and let those murderers get off free?" asked Baker.

"If you won't guarantee them a fair trial, yes, we should walk away," Bradley insisted.

"A fair trial, did my boy get a fair trial? I say they'll have their trial before God and the sooner the better. You are forgetting that he killed my son, killed at least one man yesterday and wounded three others. Do you still say we just walk away?" asked Newt Tackett.

"In all fairness, Newt, they were just trying to defend themselves yesterday when you yourself lead that ill-fated charge against the house. We have heard more than one side with your son and from what I heard about what Jack did to Mrs. Jackson, Reeves had a good reason to go gunning after him," replied Bradley uncomfortably.

"I did what you said and she deserved it. She is nothing but a whore," said Big Jack with a sneer.

Bradley ignored Jack and looked at Baker, "Big Jack is no more the legal sheriff of Twin Creeks than I am. Just because you gave him that badge, he thinks that he is a big man. And you are just doing this because Carla Jackson wouldn't marry you and you want her ranch," replied Bradley.

"Bradley, now you are getting personal. I'd suggest that you get to town and pick up your belongings and clear out because if you are still around when I get to town I'm going to kill you," yelled Baker.

"I'm leaving right now but I'll be there in town when you get back. And I don't think that you have the guts to kill anyone. That's why you have hired all of these gunmen," snapped Bradley as he turned and walked away.

As Bradley was mounting his horse he was joined by four other men. They mounted and the five of them rode out without looking back.

"Why are you allowing them to leave?" asked Big Jack. I'll bring them back with a gun dead or alive.

"Don't be a fool Jack. If we start killing townsfolk we may lose all of them. Besides, we still have plenty of men left. Let's get started."

It was becoming unbearably hot in the remains of the rock house and there was very little shade. Morgan had taken a blanket and created a small tent but it was not big enough for three people to get in. Besides if they did they would not be able to see anyone that might be coming through the passage way. Carla wiped the sweat from her brow onto her sleeve and asked, "What time do you reckon it is now?"

Morgan looked up to the sky. "By the position of the sun I'd say pretty close to noon. Unfortunately it's going to get even hotter for the next few hours. Just make sure that you drink plenty of water and you and Jamie stay inside the tent as much as possible."

"I'm going to stay out here with you. They may be coming soon."

He looked at her, "I don't know what to say Carla. I've been a fool. I should have known that when I went after Big Jack that they would take it out on you as well as me."

"Morgan, please don't blame yourself," replied Carla. "Nick Baker and Newt Tackett would have cooked up other excuses if it hadn't been you. Baker wanted to marry me and take my ranch. He figured it would be easier to marry me but when I told him no he decided to just take the ranch. It would be easier for him if I was not around and that is what he wants now."

"Why is Tackett so dead set on getting rid of you?" asked Morgan.

"Newt Tackett is a mean and vicious man. He came to the house when he found out that I needed money and wanted to buy my services. The first time he beat me and choked me in the name of sex. I had bumps and bruises all over my body. I refused to see him anymore so he has been angry ever since. The problem is that he told everyone that he was meeting me on a regular basis. That's where his son got all of his anger toward me."

Morgan shook his head, "I know that there were issues but I got you in trouble right now and gave them an excuse. The problem is now I'm not sure that I can get you out."

She looked at him and saw the anguish in his eyes. "Morgan, you have been the best thing that has come along in my life since my husband died. You haven't tried to take advantage of me even though you know what I am. I owe you an awful lot and I don't hold you responsible for what is happening to us."

"I don't understand."

Morgan, I feel that I am a lucky woman. The way you went off trying to take care of Big Jack for what he did to me. Most folks around here just think that I deserved what I got, whatever it was. Yes, I feel that I am a lucky woman."

"Carla, I don't know how lucky you are but I do know that you are a fine woman," he said.

Carla blushed deeply. "Thank you, Morgan."

No sooner had she finished speaking than the shooting started up again. Morgan again ignored the shooting but he kept his eyes on the passage way. This time men ran through the passage way firing as quickly as they could.

"Get ready, there're coming," said Morgan as he aimed the Henry and fired several rounds.

The first two shots hit the rocks and ricocheted away but the third shot found its mark and a man went down gut shot. He screamed and went down continuing to moan and groan and hollering for help.

His next shot hit a man in the leg just above his knee. He dropped down with the other man and temporarily blocked the passageway. The other men that were trying to jump over the bodies caused them to be exposed to Morgan's rifle. Another man went down and all chaos turned lose with the men behind the bodies. Baker screamed for them to retreat.

The shooting stopped and all that could be heard were the wounded men moaning and screaming. Baker didn't want the other men to be discouraged so he stepped up on a rock and hollered for silence. The men continued to talk among themselves and finally Big Jack took his pistol, aimed it toward the sky and fired three times.

"Everybody shut up, listen to Mr. Baker," hollered Big Jack.

"Thank you, Sheriff," said Baker. "Now they have out foxed us again but we still have plenty of men and I have a plan to finish this job quickly."

Several folks began talking among themselves but Baker raised his voice to get their attention. "We are going to have some sharpshooters and we are going to post them as high as we can so that when they fire we will see them and fire back. Now you all just wait for a while until we get the sharpshooters in place before you charge again."

Several of the people mumbled among themselves but moved back out of the line of fire and many sat down on the ground. Pete Cordell approached Baker. "What's on your mind, Cordell?" asked Baker.

"There are a lot of innocent people that are going to be hurt or killed before this thing is over," he said evenly.

"I'd say you'd be right but there is not much that we can do about it now can we?" he replied.

"You could let them come down and guarantee them their safety. We can allow them a fair trial. You know that they will be convicted."

"We have been down that road before. We are not going to take any chances of them going free."

"Baker, I've been with you over three years and I done a damn good job with you but I can't take part in something like this."

"You are going to take part or you will be finished in this county," he snapped.

"There is a time when a man has to stomp his own snakes. This is your fight and you are going to get a lot of people hurt that have no steak in this fight. I'm walking away."

Big Jack had been quiet but he dropped his right hand onto his pistol. "Big Jack, you drag iron and I'm gonna plug your boss and maybe you too," snapped Cordell.

"Now, Pete, we have been friends for a long time," replied Big Jack letting his hand fall away from his gun.

"Big Jack, we have never been friends, we have been acquaintances. You are a bully and a braggart but don't try and bully me because you know that I can take you in a fair draw any day," he answered calmly.

Cordell started backing up toward his horse and Big Jack took a couple steps forward. "Baker, if you want to die, you let that big baboon take another step," warned Cordell.

"Jack, you stand still. He'll do what he says," growled Baker.

"You are a smart man, Baker," he taunted him as he reached his horse. "I'm going to the ranch and gather up my things and clear out. You best not try and stop me." He mounted and rode out without incident.

A few minutes later Newly Thompson came riding in. "You got the rifles, Newly?" asked Big Jack.

"I got them," he replied as he unloaded the rifles.

"You boys give Newly a hand and get those rifles distributed to the right people so that we can get them placed where they will do the most good," commanded Big Jack.

The gunsmith gave the guns up and walked up to Baker. "I got the guns. The sights will let them hit anything that they can see," he explained with a smile.

"Good job, Newly. I knew that you could do it."

"Thanks," said Newly as he headed off toward his horse.

"Where are you going, Newly?" questioned Baker.

"I've been up all night and the riding to town and back has caused me to be tired and sleepy. I thought that I would go home and get some sleep."

"This will all be over soon and you can sleep all that you want to. We have already lost too many men we can't afford to lose any more."

"But I'm really tired . . ."

Baker looked back at him. "I think that you need to stay around and see how these rifles work."

"But . . ."

"But nothing, you're staying," Baker said now, getting angry.

The gunsmith turned and headed back to the group.

"Jack, we have to get the sharpshooters in place so that Reeves won't get a good shot, said Baker.

"Well, I've already assigned the men but it is going to take some time because the shooters will have to climb up over these rocks to get any decent shots," replied Big Jack.

"Okay, get them positioned as fast as you can and let me know when they are in place."

Chapter Twenty-seven

"Well, we got through the first round," said Morgan.

"Are we better off the longer we hold out? Are we going to get any help?" Carla asked.

"Yes, we are better off. We have killed and injured a few men so they are out of the game. Apparently the sheriff has quit the fight and I suspect others have left also. Are we going to get any help? I just don't know."

"What are they waiting for? With all of the men and the guns that they have I don't think it would be difficult to overrun our position."

"I suspect that they are hatching another strategy after we clogged up the passage way."

"They can't get up here without coming through the passageway can they?"

"It won't be easy but they could scale the rocks and get level with us or maybe even higher. If that happens we could be sitting ducks because we couldn't see the passage way and all of those folks will come through and be right on top of us."

"How long will that take?"

"It could take as long as an hour or more. The only hope we have is if they don't get in position until after dark."

"Why don't you take a short nap and I'll keep watch. I'll wake you if I hear or see anything," she said.

"Okay but no more than thirty minutes or so."

"Go ahead and I'll wake you when its time."

Since Morgan had very little sleep last night he decided that it was a good idea to get a short nap. He leaned against a rock, covered his eyes with his hat and quickly went to sleep.

§

Tom and Billy Clay reached the fork in the road that the sheriff had mentioned. They were making good time. "Bill, what do you think?" asked Tom.

"I vote that we take the short cut. It couldn't be much more difficult than what we have come through."

"Somehow I knew that you would vote for the short cut," he replied with a chuckle.

"Whatever it is, I took it from you, Pop," said Billy.

"I'd say that's a compliment. Let's ride," replied Tom.

Unfortunately, Billy was wrong. The short cut could and did get more difficult. It was a steep climb and at one point there was a rock slide and the two men thought at first that they may have to turn back. However, they knew that if that happened it was going to take them more than the eight hours. They worked for several minutes moving enough of the rocks that they could get the horses through then mounted and rode on.

They stopped only to give the horses a blow and to lead them through a couple of narrow spots. Then they had finally reached the fork at the other side.

"The sheriff said about an hour and a half from here," said Billy.

"Yes, but these horses are worn out. I think we need a ten minute rest for the horses and get them some water."

"I'm for that. I need to get off this animal and stretch," replied Billy.

They rested the horses for a few minutes and rode on. Just under two hours later they rode into the town of Twin Creeks. They had been on the road just under nine and half hours and they had plenty of daylight left.

As they rode in, it appeared that the town was deserted. Something moved off to the right and both men looked quickly. A skinny dog walked along the street looking from side to side as if it expected someone to kick him.

"I'm getting jumpy, I guess," said Tom.

"Me too," replied Billy

They moved on and stopped the horses at the livery stable and dismounted. The livery stable door was closed and Tom knocked on the door. No one answered so he tried the door and it was unlocked. They led the horses inside and unsaddled them. They brushed them down and provided grain and water for them before they left.

The two men walked directly to the sheriff's office. Tom knocked on the door. No one answered. Tom knocked on the door again, harder, but still no answer.

"No one is in the livery stable and no one in the sheriff's office. The only place that appears to be open is the saloon over there called the Red Rooster," said Billy.

"Bill, do you know any better way to get information than visiting the town saloon?"

"Can't say as I do," replied Billy

"Then we will head that way. At least we may be able to get a beer along with some information, we hope," replied Tom.

"My throat feels like it is filled with alkali dust. A beer or two could be just what the doctor ordered," remarked Billy.

They walked the few steps to the saloon and entered. The only person they saw was a man sitting with his head down at one table.

"He is dead, drunk or sleeping," suggested Billy.

Tom walked over and shook the man but he didn't move. "Bill, get me a pitcher of cold water."

"I'd prefer to get a pitcher of beer," he replied with a smile.

"There will be time for the beer later."

Billy got the water and handed it to his dad. Tom poured about half of the water over the ex-sheriff's head. The man shuddered and moaned then put his head back down on the table. Tom poured the rest of the water over his head and he came up with a start, "What the hell is going on?"

"Sorry, Friend. We are looking for the sheriff," said Tom.

"And who are you?"

"We are friends of Morgan Reeves. You know him?"

"I know him or did know him."

"What do you mean by that?" said Billy as he put his hand on the man's shoulder.

"We want answers and we want them quickly."

The sheriff reached up to get the half empty bottle of whiskey on the table but Tom grabbed it first. "I think that you have had enough for the time being."

"What do you want?"

"Listen closely. We want to find the sheriff and we want to find Morgan Reeves and we want to find them quickly."

Cal Daniels staggered out of the back room and looked at the men. "My eyes are blurry, how many of you are there? What are you doing with the sheriff?" he demanded.

"Where is the sheriff?" asked Tom.

"He's right there, oh no, he is not the sheriff anymore," replied Daniels.

Tom looked at both men for a moment then addressed Daniels, "Get us two beers and quick."

"It is not very cold."

"It doesn't matter as long as it is wet," replied Billy.

Ex-sheriff John Billings managed to stand up. "I'm the former sheriff and the man Morgan Reeves that you are looking for is about two miles from town, up on a hillside. That is if he is still alive."

"Why the hell ain't you out there with him?" snapped Billy.

"There are thirty or forty men out there and they ran me off," explained Billings.

"You are supposed to be the sheriff. You are supposed to make the decisions and call the shots," said Billy visually annoyed.

"Forget it Bill, let's get our beer, and then get going. Can you give us directions to where he is?" asked Tom.

Cal Daniels came over to the table and set down two large glasses of beer. "That should hold you for a short spell," said Daniels.

"I'll do even better, I'll take you there," said Billings.

"With all of the alcohol you have in you, are you sure that you are up to the ride?" asked Tom.

"It's my duty. I should not have given up my badge to that big baboon."

Billy had already drunk most of his beer when Tom picked up his. He drank thirstily before speaking.

"Okay, Sheriff, do you have any fresh horses? Ours are about played out," asked Tom.

"We'll just take some horses from the livery stable. No one will hang us for that," said Billings with a chuckle.

"Bill, can you get some horses from the livery stable? I'll see if I can rustle up some grub."

"I'll go with you," said Daniels.

Billy finished his beer in one big swallow and the two men left the saloon. Tom looked around and came up with some food to eat on the way.

"I'm going to get my guns from the office and I'll meet you in front of the jail in about ten minutes. By the way, who are you?"

"Tom Clay and the other one is Billy Clay my son. By the way do you have any extra shells for my Winchester?"

"Glad to meet you both. Sure I'll bring some extra ammunition with me," said the sheriff as he left the saloon, none too sturdy.

Exactly ten minutes later the four heavily armed men with fresh horses rode out of Twin Creeks.

CHAPTER TWENTY-EIGHT

Carla woke Morgan when she thought that she heard someone near. He got up and looked around but didn't see or hear anyone. He picked up one of the canteens and took a small swallow. He handed it to her and after she took a drink she gave it to Jamie who was sitting behind her, organizing the bullets. After taking a drink he handed it back to Morgan.

"We need to get ready. He looked around for possible locations for sharpshooters and pointed them out to Carla and Jamie. They also decided the best locations for hiding if in fact the shooters got in position.

"Jamie, are you ready for the ammunition when they come?" he asked.

"I'm ready. I got them all counted out," he replied.

"Good boy, now just keep your eyes peeled for anyone or anything," he cautioned.

Morgan tried to keep his eyes open but the bright sunlight and the 100 degree temperature kept him from focusing very well. He was startled when a bullet went past his head not missing him more than five or six inches. He flattened out on the rocks and the bullet ricocheted off the wall shattering rock fragments everywhere.

"Everyone okay?" he asked as he looked around at Carla and Jamie.

Seeing that they were okay he carefully lifted his head trying to find out the direction the bullet came from. Then came another shot and several more in quick succession. Morgan aimed the rifle and fired off several shots in the direction of the bullets. He was sure that he had not hit anyone because he didn't hear any hollering or screaming. He peeked his head up and looked down toward the narrow passage way. Several men were running through and heading toward the wall.

"Carla get your rifle and fire down toward the passage way. She quickly took the rifle and fired several shots toward the crowd. One of the shots hit one of Baker's men in the shoulder. The impact from the Winchester's bullet spun the man around causing him to lose his footing and tumble down the hill knocking two other men off balance and all three hitting the dirt. Men were hollering and cursing as Morgan took the Westley Richards shotgun and fired both barrels into the oncoming men. The shotgun blast hit one man in the chest knocked him down the hill and he was dead before he stopped rolling.

Morgan's blast was immediately returned. Twenty or thirty men were pouring lead into the rocks and beyond. The air was filled with the smell of burnt powder but they were just wasting their ammunition because from their position all they could see was solid rock. Carla was firing steadily into the group. One of her shots caught a man in the chest and blew a hole big enough for a man's fist to go in. He died immediately.

The men in the front were trying to fall back out of range but the other men from behind kept trying to push forward. The scene was chaotic but not much damage had been done to the mob even though Morgan and Carla had a clear shot at several of the men as they got away.

It was discouraging for Morgan because he knew that they had missed a great opportunity to cut down on the odds. In his opinion that was the only way that they could get out alive. They had to cut down enough men that they would question whether or not it was worth continuing. He figured that with Baker and Tackett together there would be little chance that they would quit. All they could do was to hang on as long as possible and pray for a miracle.

That miracle could come in the form of darkness he thought as he looked at the sun setting in the west. It would not be long until no one would be able to see. Of course that could work both ways. Out of the corner of his eye he saw a glint of metal and looked around quickly.

He saw the rifle pointed directly at him and he moved to his left as he turned, aimed and fired. The ambusher lost his rifle as it fell several feet down on the rocks. That might help a little, he thought.

Carla saw one of the sharpshooters climbing a hill directly to the west of them. She aimed the rifle and fired a quick shot but the man ducked out of sight. Jamie saw another one a few minutes later and called for Morgan. Morgan aimed the Henry and pulled the trigger chipping a rock near the man's cheek but the man was able to duck out of sight.

He looked a Carla. "We have spotted three sharpshooters but there may be more. One of them does not have a rifle so he will not be able to hurt us very bad but we still have to keep low and fire only when we have a good target. Jamie, how are we fixed with ammunition?"

"We are running low, only four shotguns shells and eight for Ma's rifle," he reported.

"We'll have to conserve ammunition so we will be able to fire when we have a really good shot," said Morgan.

He knew that if they had to wait until they only had a good target then the mob would be able to sneak up close enough that they wouldn't be able to hold them off.

"Carla you only use your rifle for the sharpshooters and use the Navy Colt if they get real close. I'm going to try and give them something else to worry about. Don't be afraid to pull the trigger."

"What are you going to do?" Carla asked with fear in her eyes.

"I'll be back soon. There is a small crevice that leads to a ledge. It appears that the ledge overlooks the camp. If I can get there and fire a few shots it may make them less willing to try and charge our position and maybe discourage some from staying around."

"Can they see you?" asked Jamie.

"I don't think so but I'll be careful. Once I fire a few shots to attract their attention in a different direction I'll get right back here."

He crawled away from them carrying only the shotgun and four shells and reached the crevice. The size was okay for a short while but then it narrowed. His knees and elbows, already sore from crawling were now raw and bleeding. He had no choice so he continued until he reached the ledge. The ledge was not as wide as he first thought and any misstep might send him plunging down the hill and into the mob of men. If the fall didn't kill him, certainly Baker's men would.

Morgan heard Carla's rifle fire three times and the last time it hit flesh and a scream from a wounded man. He leaned over the ledge as far as he could and looked down. He could only see a few of the men but that would serve his purpose anyway. He quietly pulled the hammers back on the shotgun and aimed as close to the mob as he could and fired both barrels. He heard the sounds of pain and surprise from below. After the initial surprise they started firing back at him. He knew that he didn't have enough cover so he carefully backed up through the crevice until he reached the rock house.

"I'm glad you are back. I was afraid that they would rush us while you were gone," she said.

"Well, I don't know if I helped any but I did get rid of two shotguns shells and got bloody elbows and knees in the process," he replied.

"Here let me see if I can help," she said.

"I'll be okay, let's just pay attention to the passageway and the sharpshooters. Carla, you concentrate on the passageway and shoot at anything that you see moving," explained Morgan."

"That will be easier for me to only concentrate on one target. I'm worn out and my eyes are watering from the gun smoke," she replied.

Morgan pulled off his neckerchief and poured a bit of water from a canteen onto the neckerchief. He tossed it to Carla, "Dab yours eyes it may help a little."

"Thank you Morgan."

Chapter Twenty-nine

Baker was thinking about the same topic of darkness but he figured that it might be easier for his men to sneak in their stronghold at night. The daylight attacks had been a failure even with the sharpshooters. He was sure that Reeves had not been able to sleep much and his nerves would have to be frayed by now. He called the men back from the passage way and gave them assurances that the next time that they attacked they would be successful. He kept the sharpshooters on the surrounding hills with orders to fire. They kept up a consistent firing keeping the three down with little chance to aim their weapons.

"How much longer are we going to wait?" asked Big Jack.

"It'll be dark in a couple of hours and we will move then. If we lose very many more men the rest may decide to quit and go home. We'll keep the sharpshooters firing to keep them pinned down."

"What do we do in the meantime?" asked Big Jack nervously.

"Pick a couple of our best men and move into the passageway. I want them to be careful but just see if they can draw fire without getting hit. We need to force them to use up their ammunition."

"Okay, Boss, we'll do it."

Big Jack picked a couple of men and sent them into the narrow passageway one after another. They didn't get very far when the bullets of Morgan's Henry drove them back.

"It's too hot to try and get through there. That Reeves is hell on wheels with that Henry that he carries," said Wade Cross.

"Either of you get hit?" asked Big Jack.

"I got cut from rock fragments. It's bleeding but I'll be okay," replied Joe Colder.

"Okay Joe, go on back and have someone take a look at you arm. Wade you come with me."

The walked over to where Baker and Tackett were having a conversation.

"Any progress?" asked Tackett.

"Just drawing fire," said Big Jack. "Don't you think that Reeves should be low on ammunition by now?"

"He couldn't have carried a lot of ammunition with only one horse and being in a hurry to leave," added Baker.

"Yes, and they would have had to carry it up the hill. So all that we have to do is draw their fire until they are out and then we walk in," replied Tackett with a smile on his face.

"Tackett, Reeves is not a fool. Do you think that he is just going to waste his ammunition without having a target to shoot at?" asked Baker.

"Well if I had lead the attack, we would have gotten them or forced them to use all of their ammunition by now," replied Tackett.

"If we had allowed you to lead the attack, you would have been dead and most of the townsfolk with you," Baker snapped.

"You haven't done any better," growled Tackett.

Chapter Thirty

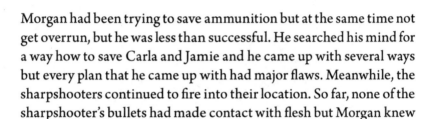

Morgan had been trying to save ammunition but at the same time not get overrun, but he was less than successful. He searched his mind for a way how to save Carla and Jamie and he came up with several ways but every plan that he came up with had major flaws. Meanwhile, the sharpshooters continued to fire into their location. So far, none of the sharpshooter's bullets had made contact with flesh but Morgan knew that it would be just a matter of time.

"Morgan, I think that we need go get some more water before it gets too dark," Carla whispered.

"Okay, you keep watch and I'll go get some."

"I'll get the water," said Jamie enthusiastically.

"Jamie, you might get hit from the sharpshooters."

"I won't, Mom, I'll be very careful."

"What do you think, Morgan?" she asked.

"He'll be all right as long as he is careful and stays down," Morgan replied.

"Okay, I'm on the way," said Jamie as he picked up two canteens and drug them with him and crawled away toward the water hole.

Morgan turned away and concentrated on the mob below. It had only been a couple of minutes when he heard a shot over his head and yell of pain from Jamie. "I'm hit."

"Jamie," hollered Carla. She started to stand up and go for Jamie but Morgan hollered for her to stay put.

"Stay still and stay down, Jamie, I'm going to come and get you," Morgan hollered back.

"I'm bleeding."

"You'll be okay, I'm coming," replied Morgan as he hurriedly crawled over to Jamie.

Morgan reached Jamie and looked at the wound. It was not a direct bullet wound but one caused by a ricocheting rock. It was a two inch gash on the fat part of the boys arm. He pulled out his hunting knife from his boot.

"Okay Jamie hold still I'm going to cut off your shirt sleeve so that I can see your arm. You're going to be okay. It's not as bad as it seems."

"It hurts Morgan, but I'm okay," Jamie assured him.

Morgan cut the shirt sleeve and looked a little closer. It was bleeding a lot but it was a clean wound. He took the sleeve and wrapped it around the arm and tied it to stop the bleeding.

"You will be okay but it will hurt some so just hang on. Can you crawl back to where your mother is?" he asked.

"Sure I can do it."

Morgan picked up the two full canteens and followed Jamie back to where Carla was lying.

"Is he going to be okay?" she asked pleadingly.

"He'll be fine as long as we can keep his arm from bleeding." he replied.

"I'll try and keep him still and quiet."

Morgan got up on his knees and looked around. He could not see anyone but he drew several rounds of bullets from the sharpshooters. He fired three shoots from the Henry in return and the fourth clicked on an empty shell. He looked over where Jamie had laid the shells and only saw two for the Henry and he knew he only had two for the shotgun. He checked his belt and found that he had no shells for the Navy Colt.

"How many bullets do you have in the pistol?"

Carla spun the cylinder and replied, "Four and I have none in the Winchester."

Morgan looked away and didn't say anything.

"We're in trouble, aren't we?" she asked.

"We're not in a bed of roses, if you know what I mean. We need one of those miracles."

"I believe in miracles," whispered Jamie.

"So do I," replied Carla.

Morgan looked at the two, "I guess that miracles do happen some times. Jamie, how do you feel?"

"I just feel tired."

"Try and get some sleep and you'll feel better when you wake up."

CHAPTER THIRTY-ONE

"Okay, Big Jack it's time to move," said Baker.

Newt Tackett, with his rifle, was right near by. "I'm ready to go."

Baker looked over at Tackett, "Keep down and don't get your fool head shot off," snapped Baker sarcastically.

"I'm surprised that you haven't already," said Big Jack with a laugh.

Tackett ignored Big Jack, moved forward into the passage way, crawling on his knees. Big Jack ordered another half dozen men to follow him.

They went firing through the passageway. Tackett ducked to the right when he got through the passageway and the man behind him took a load of buckshot in the chest from the shotgun Morgan was holding. He screamed in pain and rolled around in agony. Another man stepped over him and took a load in his legs from the second shot. Both men were screaming in pain and getting in the way of the others trying to come through the narrow passage.

§

Tom Clay led the small group of men toward the hill and heard the shooting almost a mile away. He looked back at the men, "We need to pick up the pace," and they did. When they reached a spot a few hundred yards away they reined in their mounts.

"Clay, you know they brought in rifles with special sights on them meaning they must have sharpshooters set up somewhere," said John Billings.

"That means we need to locate them before we ride into an ambush," replied Billy Clay.

"Billings, you and your friend stay here, Billy, you and I are going to circle the area and see if we can pick off the snipers. We'll leave our horses here."

Morgan fired the last of the shotgun ammo, set the gun down and picked up the Henry. He had two bullets left and Carla had four in the Navy Colt. He pulled out the hunting knife and laid it down on a rock close by. Darkness was coming and it was now difficult to see. This meant that the mob would be coming over the rock wall and they couldn't stop them.

Bullets from the sharpshooters began again and Morgan pointed the Henry in the direction of the shots but he didn't fire. And then he heard someone firing from farther away. The mob was still firing but the sharpshooter's bullets stopped. Carla heard it also. "Did you hear that? What does it mean?"

"I'm not sure but it could be that we have some help from the outside."

"Could that be your friend Tom Clay?"

"It could be or that the sheriff, John Billings, grew some courage," he replied.

Just then two men came over the wall. "Look out, Carla."

Morgan picked up his hunting knife and when the first man hit the ground Morgan stuck the knife between his ribs. He inhaled a big breath then screamed, rolled over and continued to scream. Morgan pulled out the knife and whipped the blood on the man's shirt. He heard two shots right on top of him and looked over at Carla. She had fired the Navy Colt and hit the other man in the chest but then she was holding her thigh with the blood gushing from a bullet hole.

Morgan looked at both men but neither of them was going to give them any problems. He took his knife and cut off the sleeve of his shirt and wrapped it around her thigh to stop the bleeding and went back to his post. There were no more bullets glancing off the rocks.

"Carla, do you hear that?"

"What? I don't hear anything," she replied with a confused look on her face.

"They are not shooting at us anymore," he answered.

"Who are they shooting at? They are still shooting," asked Jamie.

"I don't know who for sure but there is someone out there who is on our side," he replied.

Morgan risked a look over the rock and saw several men backing up the hill but shooting down the hill. He recognized Newt Tackett and looked for Big Jack and Nick Baker and he could see neither of them.

He stood up with the Henry and shouted, "Newt Tackett, drop the rifle and get down on the ground."

"I'm going to kill you and the whore you are with," Tackett snarled.

"You turn around and you're dead," snapped Morgan.

Tackett ignored his warning and swung around with the rifle pointed at Morgan. Morgan fired and his bullet struck the store owner in the chest. Tackett pulled the trigger of his rifle but it harmlessly struck a rock a few feet away. He grunted and dropped to the ground. The man next to Tackett screamed in fear. "I give up, I quit I'm putting down my gun. Don't shoot."

"Throw down your gun and get down on the ground," hollered Morgan.

Another man screamed out surrender followed by another and another. Pretty soon all of the remaining men had given up.

"Where are Big Jack and Nick Baker?" hollered Morgan.

No one answered and Morgan asked the question again louder.

"They both got on their horses and rode away a few minutes ago," answered one of the men on the ground.

"What direction did they ride?"

"West toward Sweetwater," replied another man.

"Was it just the two of them?" asked Morgan.

"There were at least four or five men rode out with them."

Morgan ran back to where Carla was sitting with her back to a rock. Jamie was sitting with her.

"Are you two okay?"

"We will both be fine," Carla answered. "Here is your gun."

"I'm going after Big Jack," said Morgan.

"Morgan, let him go. It's not worth you getting hurt," she pleaded.

"He has to pay for all of the things that he has done."

"Go ahead, Morgan. I'll take care of everything here." Morgan turned around and saw sheriff John Billings along with Tom and Billy Clay.

"Hello, Morgan, you old son of a gun, it's good to see you again. I figured that we would have to bury your ornery carcass," said Tom Clay.

Morgan shook hands warmly with all three men. "Tom, Billy, what are you two sidewinders doing over here?"

"We're here to rescue you from a tiny group of men out there," replied Tom.

"I didn't need any help from you two, we were doing just fine," said Morgan with a laugh.

"Sure, you allowed me and Jamie both to get shot. How many bullets do you have in that rifle?" asked Carla.

"Oh, I think one. Tom, Billy I want to introduce you to Carla Jackson and the bravest gent I've ever known, Jamie Jackson."

"Ma'am, glad to meet you. Howdy, Jamie," said Tom.

"Me too, Big Man," added Billy as he patted Jamie on the back.

"I'm really glad that you could make it. We had no idea how we were going to get out alive," said Carla.

"Lets save the jawing, I've some men to find," said Morgan.

"Morg, you're not going by yourself. Billy and I are going to tag along to keep you out of more trouble," replied Tom.

"Shucks, that is just two more people that I will have to protect," said Morgan with a smile.

"Sheriff, can you get these two into town and get them a room at the hotel? I'll be back as soon as I can."

"Morgan, we don't have any money for food or a hotel room."

"Carla, forget it, the town owes you and I think that the good sheriff will see to it that it happens," said Morgan as he looked over at the sheriff.

"You bet I will," replied the sheriff sheepishly.

"All right men let's ride toward Sweetwater," said Morgan.

Morgan picked out a stout bay horse from the group of horses left over. He rounded up some bullets for his Navy Colt and the Henry and the three men headed for the town of Sweetwater. It was too dark to try and track Baker and his men so he decided to take the word of Baker's man and go straight to Sweetwater.

CHAPTER THIRTY-TWO

Although it was now dark, the three men started toward the town of Sweetwater with Morgan Reeves leading the way.

"You familiar with the layout of Sweetwater?" asked Tom.

"Sort of, but I've only been there once and it was a few days ago and only for a few hours. I went after supplies for Carla and Jamie," replied Morgan.

"Don't tell me, the folks in Twin Creeks wouldn't sell her any," replied Billy.

"You got it. The town was shut down tight as far as she was concerned, even when she had money."

"We came through also. We met Benson, the sheriff. He appeared to be a good man," reported Tom. "He said that you had stopped by."

"Yes, stopped by his office while I was there but they told me he was out of town."

"Are we planning on riding through or camping before we get there?" asked Billy.

"We are going to ride as far as we can but there is some rough country between here and there, we'll have to be very careful. There is a little bluff overlooking the town. I'd planned on camping there then ride on in early the next morning. Hopefully we can get far enough to get a couple hours of sleep before morning."

"I agree the best time to face them would be early in the morning. How many men are we looking at facing?" asked Tom.

"Well the man said four or five that would mean seven. However, Baker had at least twelve men at his ranch at one point. At least half a dozen of them are dead or wounded," replied Morgan.

It was nearly two o'clock in the morning when the three men reached the bluff overlooking Sweetwater. They dismounted, unsaddled their horses and staked them out so that they could get water and grass. Without building a fire, they spread their saddle blankets and went to sleep.

§

After a hard ride, Baker and his five men rode into the town of Sweetwater. Their first stop was the Sweetwater Saloon. They tied their horses at the hitching rail and stepped up on the sidewalk. "I'm going to have one drink and then check into the hotel. I'd suggest that you all do the same. We are going to be up early in the morning," said Baker.

"You buying?" asked Big Jack.

"I'm buying the first one, any more is at your expense and at your risk if you are not up early," ejaculated Baker as he and the men walked inside. They took a place at the bar. Baker ordered whiskey while the other men ordered beer.

"What's the plan?" asked Big Jack.

"Tomorrow we are going to have breakfast and then ride back to the ranch," replied Baker.

"Do you think that Reeves and the ex-sheriff will be riding after us?" asked Wade Cross.

"I'm not sure about Billings but there will be no doubt that Reeves will be after us. We'll have to deal with him sooner or later."

"I should have plugged Billings when I had a chance," exclaimed Big Jack.

"You do that and the townsfolk would have turned against us. We were trying to make sure that it was all as legal as possible."

"What are we going to do about him now?" he inquired.

"We're going to kill him, how ever we have to do it. Give the men another drink and make sure that they get to sleep," said Baker as he finished his whiskey, dropped some coins on the bar and left the saloon.

CHAPTER THIRTY-THREE

It was a cool and quiet morning when Morgan Reeves, Tom Clay and Billy Clay rode into Sweetwater. The only sound that could be heard was the hammer on the anvil as the blacksmith began his work day. They headed directly to the marshal's office. When they walked inside they saw a young man sitting behind the marshal's desk with his feet propped up and dozing off.

"Good morning," greeted Tom Clay, "we're looking for Marshall George Benson."

The young man quickly jumped up from the chair, "I wasn't asleep, I was just resting."

"Young man, we are not concerned about you sleeping on duty, we are looking for the Marshall," replied Morgan.

"Oh, yeah, he would be in the café about this time. I'm Jody. The marshal lets me work here sometimes."

"Okay, Jody, much obliged for the information," said Morgan as he turned to leave the office.

"Mister, please don't tell the Marshal."

"Jody, your secret is safe with us but if you are interested in being a lawman, you better learn to be alert at all times," said Tom.

"Thank you, Sir, I'll remember that," he replied nervously.

The three men filed out of the marshal's office and stood on the sidewalk. Morgan pulled out his Bull Durham bag and rolled a cigarette then passed it to Tom.

"I don't think that young man has the gumption to become a lawman," said Billy dryly.

Tom Clay looked at his son and smiled. "I can remember when folks said the same thing about you and your brother."

Billy looked over a Morgan sheepishly and Morgan said, "Don't look at me, I agree with your father."

"Okay, I guess that I deserved that. Let's head for the café, I really am starving," replied Billy.

The two older men laughed and followed the younger man to the café. Morgan was glad that Tom could smile while talking about both of his sons.

They reached the café and walked through the door. Marshal George Benson was sitting at a table enjoying some ham and eggs. He stood up and motioned the three men to join him at his table.

"Have a seat, Gents," said the marshal. "I see that you found your way to Twin Creeks."

"Sure did and right on time. Marshal Benson this is Morgan Reeves, a good friend of mine and a former lawman," replied Tom.

The two men shook hands and everyone took a seat. "Reeves, I understand that you were in a tough spot over near Twin Creeks, how did you manage to get yourself extricated?" asked Marshal Benson.

"It's a long story and I don't think that I can tell it on an empty stomach," replied Morgan.

They waited until the waitress took their orders and brought cups and coffee for the three men. Morgan filled the marshal in on his past with Tom and Billy Clay while they waited for their food. When the food came they ate hungrily. When the food was gone Morgan explained the situation with Nick Baker and his men.

"So you think that these men are here in Sweetwater?" inquired Marshal Benson.

"We are quite sure that he came here last night with at least five of his men. We trailed them but we camped just out of town. We figured we would be better off if we came in during daylight," explained Morgan.

The marshal drained his coffee cup and asked, "I'm familiar with Nick Baker but not the others, and I would probably not recognize them. How can I help you gents?"

"Well, we don't want any innocent folks to get hurt or killed so we would prefer to confront them outside of town. They will know my face and neither of these two would recognize any of them. If you could just locate them and then let us know where they are we would greatly appreciate it," replied Morgan.

A man walked into the café, stopped, and looked directly at the three men at the table. Morgan turned and recognized the man immediately. He stood and motioned the man over to the table.

"Hello, Dusty," said Morgan.

"Mr. Reeves, glad to see that you got away with your scalp intact," he said with a smile. "I wasn't sure that you would welcome me."

"I heard that you tried to clear up the incident at the Jackson Ranch but Baker wouldn't hear it. Marshal, have you met Dusty Metcalf?"

"I have not formally been introduced but I have seen him around the last couple of days. Good to meet you, Dusty."

"Dusty, these are Tom and Billy Clay, good friends of mine."

Tom and Billy stood up and shook hands. "You looking for Nick Baker and his gunmen?" asked Dusty.

"We are," replied Morgan.

"I saw him leaving the hotel this morning. He had five men with him, including Big Jack Coleman."

"That's what we needed to know. Did you happen to see what direction they went when they rode out?" asked Morgan.

"No, but I'd think that they were heading back to the ranch," replied Dusty.

"Thanks, Dusty."

"Mr. Reeves, let me have a talk with the blacksmith he is always the first man awake in the mornings. I don't doubt Dusty's story but it could be a trick to lead you off trail," said the marshal. "Meet me at my office in about fifteen minutes."

"Sounds good to me, Marshal," replied Morgan.

The marshal left the café and Dusty took a seat at the table and ordered breakfast while the other three finished their coffee.

"I'd be glad to help you but I'm not really a gunman," said Dusty.

"Don't worry about it, Dusty. Just stay away from the ranch," replied Morgan.

"Don't worry, I have no intentions of going anywhere near the Baker Ranch," he assured Morgan.

A few minutes later Morgan shook hands with Dusty and left some coins on the table for their breakfast. Then the three men headed for the marshal's office.

Twenty minutes or so later the marshal strode into his office. "Dusty was right, Gents. Baker and his men rode out early. According to the desk clerk they checked out around 7:00," explained Marshal Benson.

"What direction did they ride?" inquired Morgan.

"I spoke with the blacksmith and he reported that they rode north. I asked him for sure because I know that Bakers ranch is east of here but he was positive."

"That means to me that they didn't want to meet anyone coming in. Baker would figure that he would be better off at his ranch to make a stand rather than on the road" replied Morgan.

"That could also mean that he has additional men at the ranch," suggested Tom Clay.

"I'd bet on that," said Morgan.

"Well times a wastin', let's get after them," said Billy.

"We are going after them but we are going to Twin Creeks before we hit the Baker Ranch," said Morgan.

"That appears to be wasted time. I understood that the ranch was between here and Twin Creeks," replied Billy.

"Billy, what I think that Morg is saying is that we need information before we attack the ranch," explained Tom.

"It would help if we knew how many men Baker has and how heavily armed they are. Also, we may be able to get some help from Sheriff Billings," explained Morgan.

"I'd be glad to ride with you fellars but I have no jurisdiction in that area anyway."

"We appreciate it but I think we can handle it. Hope to see you down the road, Marshal," said Morgan.

CHAPTER THIRTY-FOUR

The three men rode hard and by the time they reached Twin Creeks it was getting late in the day. They went directly to the sheriff's office and walked in. Billings was sitting at his desk drinking coffee and wearing his badge.

"Come on in men. How about some coffee? I just made a fresh pot," asked the sheriff.

"I'd love some," replied Morgan.

"Me too," added Tom.

"None for me thanks, I'd rather have something stronger," said Billy.

"In due time, Son," replied Tom. Billy looked disappointed but he didn't say anything.

The sheriff brought two cups and the pot of coffee to the desk. He instructed the men to have a seat. He poured the coffee and handed one to Morgan and one to Tom Clay.

"Reeves, I would like to apologize to you for my previous actions. I dishonored my badge and I plan to give it up as soon as this situation is cleared up," said the sheriff sadly.

"That's all behind us now. I'd say let's just move on," said Morgan.

"It might be easy for you to say but I have worn this badge for twelve years. However, for the last eighteen months I have been basically an employee of Nick Baker and not the town," ejaculated the sheriff.

"Sheriff, forgive me for butting in but I wore a badge a couple of years more than you have and we lawman face temptations every day.

This country needs good lawmen and in spite of your failures you can do a service to the town if you want to," responded Tom Clay.

"Well I'm not so sure."

"Listen to him, Sheriff. Tom is one of the finest lawmen that ever wore a badge. Just think about it and you can make your decision after this is over. And don't just make it by yourself, the town will help you," argued Morgan.

"I'll think about it. By the way, that big roan horse you rode came into town. I had him put up in the livery stable."

"I sure am glad of that. I have become really fond of that big nag," responded Morgan. "Now let's get this job done."

"You know that Wade Cross came to town a couple of hours ago. He bought some supplies and ammunition. I assume that you didn't catch up to them in Sweetwater," said the sheriff.

"Apparently they just went to Sweetwater to throw us off the trail. They left bright and early in the morning. We assumed that they rode back to the ranch," replied Morgan.

"Sheriff, how many men does Baker have at the ranch?" asked Tom.

The sheriff scratched his chin and thought about it for a moment. "My best guess is that he had twelve men to begin with and five of them are down at the morgue along with another ten men. One man, Dusty, left after a dispute with Baker so I'd say six or maybe seven."

"Sheriff, we met Dusty at Sweetwater. Who are the most dangerous men with Baker?" asked Tom.

"I'd say that Wade Cross is the best man with a rifle. In fact he may be the best around. Joey Holgram is the best with a pistol but Big Jack Coleman is the meanest and probably the most dangerous."

"How about Baker? I know that he shoots off his mouth but what about his skills with a gun?" asked Morgan.

"He's a pretty fair hand with a gun but he likes to have other men do his dirty work. When are you going after Baker?" the sheriff asked.

"In the morning, are you riding with us?" asked Morgan.

"You know that I am. I'll be in my office early. Just come by and pick me up."

"We'll be here. By the way, how is Mrs. Jackson and Jamie doing?" asked Morgan.

"They are both doing okay. The doctor treated both of them and they are at the hotel, compliments of the hotel and the town. Some things have changed for the better already and with Tackett dead, it should get even better," responded the sheriff.

"Once Baker and Big Jack are dealt with, this place may become a livable town," added Morgan. He stood up, "Tom, Billy, I'm going over to the hotel and get rooms for the night. I'll meet you at the Red Rooster for a drink in about thirty minutes then we'll find some supper. Sheriff, we'd be glad for you to join us," said Morgan.

Billy grinned and said, "Sounds great to me. I have a powerful thirst. Are you sure that you don't mind me talking to your woman?"

"You know, Billy, somehow I just knew that was coming," replied Tom. "Come on, Son, let's go get a drink."

"Reeves, thanks for the invite but I'll have to beg off but I'll see you in the morning," said the sheriff.

Morgan nodded to the sheriff and walked across the street to the hotel. He entered the lobby and stepped up to the counter.

The clerk, a skinny slip of a man with a high-pitched nasal voice said, "Good evening, Mister, what can I do for you?

"I need three rooms, replied Morgan."

"Sorry, Mister, I only have one room left."

"Mister you better not be joshing me because I'm not in the mood," snapped Morgan.

"No sir, I'm not joshing you," he stammered.

"Mister Reeves, we have an extra room."

Morgan turned around and saw Carla and Jamie standing on the stairwell. He quickly walked over to them. "Are you okay?" asked Morgan as he took her hand.

"We are both fine," she replied.

"Morgan, look at my arm, I got a bandage," exclaimed Jamie.

Morgan looked at the boy and examined his arm. "That is a very nice bandage too," he replied.

"Do you want the room, Mister?"

"Look, Mr. Reeves, Jamie and I can stay in the same room so you can have his room."

Morgan hesitated only for a moment, "Okay, I'll take the room."

"We are going to eat at the Rode House Café," said Jamie. "Would you like to go?"

"I would like to but I have a couple of friends that I need you to meet first. I'll tell you what, you go ahead and I'll meet you there later. That is if it is okay with your mother," replied Morgan.

"We'd love for you to join us," responded Carla.

The three left the hotel. Morgan headed toward the Red Rooster saloon, while Carla and Jamie headed toward the café.

Morgan walked in the saloon and immediately headed over toward Tom and Billy's table.

"Have a seat, Morg," said Tom. "Bartender, bring our friend a beer. Any luck with the rooms?"

"Yes, but the two of you will have to share a room."

"We can handle that," replied Tom.

The bartender brought Morgan a beer. "Mr. Reeves, glad to see that you are still alive."

"Cal, I heard you using that shotgun out there in the hills. My question is did you hit anything?" kidded Morgan.

"I was drunk so of course I hit something. I do my best shooting when I'm drunk," ejaculated Daniels.

"And when were you not drunk?" asked Morgan with smile.

"If I remember, I'll let you know," replied Daniels as he walked back to the bar.

Morgan drained his beer. "I'm meeting with a young lady and a young man for supper. Would you two gents like to join us?" asked Morgan.

Tom looked over at Billy. "I think that Billy wants another beer so we'll have something to eat later. We'll probably meet you for breakfast."

"Don't stay up to late," joked Morgan. "And by the way Billy, can you put up the horses at the livery stable before you have too many beers?"

"I know. I'm the youngest so I'll take care of the horses. And of course we'll be ready in the morning. Just make sure that you are ready," replied Billy.

"Mind you manners toward your elders," laughed Morgan as he left the saloon.

When Morgan reached the café Carla and Jamie were already eating. He ordered beef stew, biscuits and coffee.

"What are you going to do now?" asked Carla uneasily.

"We're going after Baker and Big Jack and whoever gets in our way tomorrow morning."

"Are you taking the sheriff with you?"

"Yes, he volunteered to ride with us. We are planning to take Baker and his gunmen alive if possible."

"Morgan, you know that they are not going to give up and you may get hurt," she responded.

"I'm going to try and make sure that I don't get hurt but there is always a risk."

"You don't have to go," said Jamie.

"Yes, I have to Jamie. Someone has to do it."

Morgan's food came and he ate hungrily. After supper he escorted Carla and Jamie back to the hotel. His room, number eight, was on the second floor and had two windows. One overlooked the square across a narrow balcony and the second offered an uninspiring view of the express office. The room had undecorated walls enclosing a hard double bed, a bureau with a small mirror above it, a built-in closet and a small table with a wash basin. Nothing else except some dingy drapes on the windows. He sat down on the bed and completely cleaned the rifle and handgun then stood the Henry in the corner near the door.

The atmosphere in the room felt hot and smelled stale so Morgan opened the balcony window to admit what breeze that he could get. Although the breeze was faint it helped a little. He took off his gun and holster and put the Navy Colt under his pillow. He walked to the wash basin washed his hands and face and toweled down. He slipped off his boots and his shirt, blew out the lamp and lay down across the bed. Soon he was asleep.

He didn't know how long he had been sleeping but he came awake because of a noise. At first he thought that it came from the door but then he realized that it was coming from the window. He reached under his pillow and pulled out the Navy Colt and quickly rolled off the bed and crouched behind the bed. Two shots were fired into the bed that he had just vacated. He peered over the bed and saw the outline of a man and fired three shots instantly. A man screamed and fell back out of the window.

A few moments later a loud knock came on the door and someone hollered, "You okay, Morg?"

He recognized the voice of Tom Clay. "Come on in, I'm okay."

Tom Clay rushed through the door followed by Billy. He walked directly to the window and looked out. "You've got a body out here and I don't think that it is going to move by itself," he announced.

"What's going on in there?" asked a voice from the hallway.

"Get the sheriff," hollered back Morgan.

"Are you alright, Morgan?" hollered Carla.

"I'm fine. Stay in your room and lock the door until I tell you to open it," called back Morgan.

He struck a match and lit the lamp and looked around. The window had been broken out and the wind blew the curtains through the open window. A few minutes later the sheriff came in the room.

"What's going on?" he asked.

"We got a body outside the window," responded Tom.

The sheriff picked up the lamp and carried it to the window and leaned out. He stared at the body and turned around, "That's Dave Usher, one of Baker's men," announced the sheriff.

"I heard a horse and rider leaving town on a dead run," said Billy Clay. "That might have been another of his men."

"I'd say you'd be right. Baker usually doesn't take chances, two men against one would be fair in his estimation," said the sheriff.

"Well, there is one thing good about this," said Billy.

"And just what would that be?" asked Tom.

"One less person we have to deal with in the morning," he replied.

"Can't argue with that," responded Morgan.

The body of Dave Usher was removed to the morgue. Tom and Billy Clay went back to their room and Morgan went to Carla's room to say good night.

"Morgan, why don't you sleep in our room? It'll be safer," said Carla.

"That's not appropriate," answered Morgan.

"You don't understand, my reputation cannot get any worse."

"Your reputation is fine with me," Morgan replied. "Look I'll see you both in the morning before we leave."

"Okay then, good night, be careful," she said.

"Good night, Morgan," added Jamie.

"Good night," answered Morgan as he left the room and walked down the hallway to his own room.

Chapter Thirty-five

Even though it was early in the morning, Morgan stopped by Carla's room and spoke to Carla and Jamie. Then he met Tom and Billy Clay and they left the hotel and walked to the café. Sheriff Billings was already having breakfast when the three men entered. They all finished breakfast, walked to the livery stable and saddled their horses. Morgan was delighted to see his big roan horse. The animal nuzzled Morgan and tried to nip his hand but Morgan swatted him gently and threw the saddle on his back.

A few minutes later the four men were riding toward the Baker Ranch. The sun had just cleared the trees and a haze hovered over the creek as they walked their horses over the wooden bridge. Morgan looked up and saw just a hint of rain in the air.

"Sheriff, since you are the only one who has been at Baker's Ranch, can you give us a lowdown on the layout?" asked Morgan.

"The ranch is close to a hill with a creek some hundred yards before you reach the house. There is a wooden bridge leading up to the house. Anyone in the house or nearby would hear us coming minutes before we get there. The bunkhouse is off to the right. You could get in a cross fire if you get too close to the ranch house."

"Any way to get behind the house and surprise them?" questioned Tom.

"It's possible but the hill behind it is steep," replied the sheriff.

"How about the bunk house?" asked Morgan.

"You could get behind the bunk house by following the creek but there are no windows or doors behind it."

"That means that we ride straight in?" asked Billy.

"No, Billy. I've got another idea. I'll explain it to you when we get close to the ranch," said Morgan.

The sheriff lead the men toward the ranch with Billy Clay taking up the rear. They had just left a wooded area and headed into a draw when shots were fired from off their right side. The horses shied away, Billy yelled, fell off his horse, rolled over and lay still. The other men dismounted and raced to Billy's side. Morgan grabbed him by the shoulders and Tom took his legs and dragged him behind a boulder as the shots came again. Morgan opened Billy's shirt and examined the wound. "He's going to need a doctor and quick," exclaimed Morgan.

"They've got us pinned down. How are we going to get him out of here?" asked the sheriff.

"We are going after those bushwhackers and then get Billy back to town," snapped Tom.

"Tom, you stay here and take care of Billy. Sheriff, I want you to see how many bullets you can put in that thicket when I run toward that rock over yonder."

"We'll both do it," said Tom as he pointed his Winchester repeating rife.

Morgan pulled his Navy Colt out of the holster and spun the cylinder making sure that he had six bullets. "Okay, I'm going," said Morgan as he crouched and ran as fast as he could for the rock.

Behind him he could hear the sheriff and Tom firing as quickly as they could. He stole a glance in the thicket and saw two guns firing about fifty feet apart. Two ambushers he decided. The ambushers had seen him running and had changed their aim toward Morgan. A bullet caught his shirt sleeve and burned his right arm. Another shot hit him in the leg before he could reach the rock. He looked at his leg and saw that it was bleeding but he thought it was just a scratch.

He sprinted the last few feet, reached a stand of trees and disappeared from the ambushers sight. He came out of the trees within sight of the first ambusher. He crawled within about thirty feet of the gunman.

"Drop the gun, Mister, unless you want to be buried out here," snapped Morgan.

The startled gunman turned quickly and snapped off a shot that missed Morgan badly but Morgan's first shot hit the man in the shoulder and the second one hit him high in the chest. The man slowly slumped to the ground. Morgan quickly covered the distance between the two and examined the man. He was dead. He stood up and heard a horse galloping away from the scene.

"Everyone okay down there?" hollered Morgan.

"The two of us are okay but we need to get Billy to town quickly," answered Tom.

Morgan quickly rejoined them. "Can he stay on a horse?"

"I don't think so, we'll have to hold him on," replied Tom.

"Sheriff, ride as quickly as you can to town and get the doctor. Meet us as quickly as he can get here," said Morgan.

"Right away, by the way, who is the man you killed?" asked the Sheriff.

"Didn't recognize him, of course I didn't know all of Baker's men."

The sheriff mounted and raced down the road toward Twin Creeks. Morgan and Tom got Billy on his horse and rode on both sides to hold him in the saddle. Billy was weak and getting weaker.

"Morgan, if we ride too quickly if may kill him and if we don't hurry he may die anyway."

"Let's just keep going and hope that the sheriff can find the doctor and get him here fast."

Billy moaned, coughed and swayed. It took a lot of effort to keep him in the saddle. They continued to ride and sometime later Morgan heard horses and voices. The three men moved off the road, found cover and waited with guns drawn. Several minutes later a horse ridden by Sheriff John Billings and a buckboard came into sight. "Sheriff, looks like you made good time," hollered Morgan.

"We were lucky the doctor was leaving town to look in on another patient when I got there. Reeves, Clay this is Doctor Vance Pickard," explained the sheriff.

The doctor looked at the two men, turned away, then turned back toward Morgan like he was going to say something, but didn't. "Get the man on the ground so that I can see him," he barked.

They laid Billy on a blanket and covered him up to his waist. The doctor examined him for several minutes then turned back to Tom Clay. "The shoulder wound has bled a lot but it can be fixed easily, however the chest wound will be more difficult."

"He'll be okay, won't he?" asked Tom anxiously.

"Can't tell until I get the bullet out," he replied as he opened his bag and brought out his instruments.

"Should we take him to town before you try and take out the bullet?" asked the sheriff.

"Even in the buggy he'll be tossed around and it may kill him. I need to do it now."

"What do you want us to do?" asked Tom.

The doctor looked at the three men. "Reeves I want you to hold him down while I take out the bullet. Sheriff, get some water and then stand guard. Tom, walk over there and see if there is any trout in that stream."

"But I . . ."

"Just go ahead, Tom, we'll take care of Billy," urged Morgan.

Tom didn't say anything but he turned and walked toward the stream. Doctor Pickard expertly removed the bullet from Billy's chest and bandaged him up. "With luck and some really good care I'd say that he will be fine in a couple of weeks or so," he said.

"Tom, come on over here. We got good news," hollered Morgan.

"Let's get him in the buggy and get him back to town," said the doctor.

Tom quickly walked back from the stream and looked at Billy. He then turned around and faced Morgan. "There ain't no damn trout in that stream," he growled.

They lifted Billy and loaded him on the doctor's buggy and covered him up before the doctor climbed on. "Are you gentleman coming with me?"

"Sheriff, you and Tom head for town and help take care of Billy. I'm going to look around here," said Morgan.

"I think that I need to go along with you. You are going to need some help," said Tom.

"I don't want anyone else to get hurt. I'm going to take care of this by myself."

"Morgan, you can't do that."

"Tom, you've got Billy to take care of and the sheriff has a town to take care of and I have no one to take care of except Nick Baker and Big Jack," he argued. Now get going. You all don't have time to discuss this any more." He mounted the big roan and rode toward the Baker Ranch.

As he rode he wondered if they had posted lookouts and if so where. He drew the Navy Colt from the holster, replaced the empty rounds and slipped it back into the holster. He then pulled the Henry out of the scabbard from the saddle and checked the ammunition and held it in his hands. After he had ridden for about a half hour he reined in the roan and looked around. He pulled out his sack of Bull Durham and built a cigarette, lit it and put out the match. After a few moments he turned the horse and rode into the woods. Since it was getting late he decided that it would be better if he camped out and rode in early in the morning.

Morgan dismounted from the big roan, stripped off the saddle and bridle and tied him where he could eat and drink. He didn't have much in the way of grub but he had coffee and beef jerky. He built a small fire in a secluded area and made coffee. He ate beef jerky and drank two cups of coffee. By that time it was dark and getting colder. Keeping the fire going was a risk so he put it out and covered the ashes. The horse's blanket would keep him from freezing so he curled up and went to sleep.

He woke early, tended to the horse and made coffee. He took the last biscuit that Carla had made a few days ago and ate it along with some jerky. He washed it down with the coffee, put out the fire and saddled the roan. He stepped into the saddle and headed toward the Baker Ranch.

Several minutes later he came out of the woods and saw Baker's ranch about three hundred yards away. He stopped the roan and dismounted leading the horse to a tree where he tied him down to a limb. He peered out toward the ranch house but he could not see anyone. He walked boldly across the clearing and stopped behind a cottonwood. He listened carefully but heard nothing.

He crouched under the cottonwood tree and cocked his head, still listening. Over his head he heard the rustling of the wind and the rubbing together of two limbs. They made a dull and lonesome sound.

He heard no other sounds; his tense nerves had deceived him. He straightened and then tensed again. He heard the sound of a horse in Baker's barn. He relaxed again and studied the surroundings. The barn was about twenty-five yards away and just on the other side of the creek that the sheriff mentioned. If he could reach the creek and drop down into it he could get close to the barn or the bunk house without being seen. He crawled toward a clearing by the creek and almost made it when he heard a horse coming toward the ranch house. He was too far to turn around and too far to make the ditch. He turned, dropped the Henry and faced the rider.

"Well, well, if it isn't Morgan Reeves," the man said as he stepped down and away from his horse.

"As I remember I'd say that you would be Joey Holgram," replied Morgan.

"And I understand that you are pretty good with that gun you carry in that holster," replied Holgram.

"I have heard the same about you but I'm not interested in drawing on you. I'm looking for Big Jack and Nick Baker. You can just turn around and keep riding and we'll have no quarrel."

"Reeves, I ride for the brand. That means that if the ranch is in trouble, so am I."

"Even if it means that you die for the brand?"

"Even if it means that I die, but I don't think that I will be the one to die."

"That's too bad that you feel that way," said Morgan.

"It's too late to avoid it Reeves, let's get it done," replied Holgram. "I can't wait to even the score from the gun butt you gave me the first time we met."

"Holgram, you asked for it the first time and you are asking for it again. If you are sure then go ahead and make your move," said Morgan.

Holgram was fast but not fast enough. Morgan's bullets hit him in the chest and he crumpled to the ground. He was still alive but just barely. Morgan kneeled down close to Holgram, "How many men are in that house?" he asked.

"I ride for the brand, I can't, I can't tell . . ." He took a last breathe and expired.

Just as Morgan stood he heard someone yell and bullets came flying past his head. He picked up the Henry, turned and ran toward the tree that he had started from. He reached the tree and turned around looking at the house. Three men were mounting their horses and heading toward the wooden bridge. He leveled a shell in the chamber of the Henry and fired several shots back at the three men. Without waiting to see the effects of his shots he turned and sprinted toward his horse.

He unfastened the reins, jumped into the saddle and rode away from Baker's Ranch. He was not really familiar with the area so he just rode watching over his shoulder for any of Baker's men. He had ridden for about an hour when he reined in the big roan for a brief rest and a look back over his trail. He couldn't see or hear anyone. He took out his sack of Bull Durham and rolled a cigarette. He struck a match, lit the cigarette and broke the match putting the pieces into his pocket. He inhaled the smoke deeply and blew it out. He made a decision. He was not going to run any farther.

Chapter Thirty-six

Morgan swung the big roan around and back-tracked. After a few minutes of riding the roan nickered softly. He turned the horse quickly and rode him behind a clump of trees. He dismounted and moved to the front of the roan. He put one of his hands over the horse's nose to keep him quiet. Two men came into sight. Where was the third man that he saw leaving the ranch? He waited until the two men passed and stepped out behind them.

"Hold it right there, Gents," snapped Morgan.

"Who are you and what do you want?" asked one man.

"I want you both to raise your left hands and turn those horses around facing me, and be very careful."

They turned around and faced Morgan. "Morgan Reeves, we meet again."

"Wade Cross, yes we meet again," replied Morgan.

"What do you want, Mister?" asked the other rider.

"Reeves, that's Garr Madison," replied Wade. "He is a dangerous man with a gun."

"Cross, I have nothing against either of you. My problem is with Baker and Coleman. All that I want is for you both to ride out," explained Morgan.

"Reeves, you know that we can't do that . . ."

"Let me guess, you ride for the brand. Are you ready to die for the brand?" he asked.

"In case you have not noticed, Reeves, there are two of us and we both can use a gun," responded Madison.

"Lots of people who can use a gun die quickly," said Morgan.

"There is a bounty on your head and I expect to claim it," snarled Madison.

"How about you Cross, are you going to try to claim the bounty?" asked Morgan.

"Cross hesitated for a moment. He looked at Madison and then at Morgan. "I'm riding out. I think that I would like to live a little longer."

"Cross, I never figured you for a coward," sneered Madison.

"Call me whatever you want but I'll still be alive," he answered as he turned his horse and rode away.

"Now it's up to you, Madison."

Without saying a word Madison reached for the gun at his side. With lightening speed Morgan reached for the Navy Colt and fired one time hitting Madison in the chest. He folded up and dropped out of the saddle hitting the ground with a thud. Morgan examined his body but he was already dead. He was not sure how many men Baker still had but he knew that he had one less than he had yesterday.

§

Nick Baker was livid. "Jack, can't you and your men do anything right?"

"We're doing all that we can."

"The hell you say, Wade Cross and Dave Usher were sent to take care of Reeves in town only to have Cross come back empty handed and Usher dead. On top of that you sent two men to ambush him on the way to the ranch and one of them came back empty handed and the other is dead. And now Joey Holgram is dead, shot less than two hundred yards from the house. That's the best you can do? And why did Luther come back to the ranch?"

"His horse threw a shoe and he had to come back. I told him to stay around."

"Do you think that was wise?"

"Boss, I'm sure that Cross and Madison will get him and bring him back alive or dead."

"You better be right. How many men do we still have here on the ranch?"

"Counting old Henry?"

"No. you know that he can't do anything."

"Then we have two plus you and I."

"We need to keep them around close to the house until we can take care of Reeves."

"I'll take care of him myself, if you allow me to," said Big Jack.

"Jack, I know that you could beat him to death with your fists but I doubt that Reeves is going to let you get that close to him."

"I can use a gun."

"So could Holgram, he was better with a handgun than you are and now he is dead."

"Then what do we do now?" he asked.

"I want you and Luther to go after Cross and Madison, get them back here and don't go anywhere near town," he ejaculated.

"I'll get Luther and we'll ride."

Big Jack walked to the bunk house where Luther Beck and Herb Slocum were playing cards. "Luther, did you get your horse shoed?"

"Yep, that's the first thing I did when I got back."

"Good, get him saddled, we are going to take a ride. Slocum, keep your gun ready in case Reeves comes back."

Twenty minutes later Big Jack and Luther Beck came upon the body of Garr Madison.

"Hold up a minute," said Big Jack as he dismounted.

Luther stayed in the saddle while Big Jack examined the body. When he found that he was dead he searched the man's pockets and found seventeen dollars. He pocketed the money and walked back to his horse.

"You took his money," questioned Luther, "is he dead?"

"Sure, I'm taking it. He's not going to be in need of the money anymore."

"Well he's dead, but where is Cross?" asked Luther.

"It's doesn't appear that he is around here anywhere and his horse went that direction," said Big Jack, pointing north.

"How do you know that the tracks you are looking at belong to Cross?

"You see that left front track. It is wider than the others. It is caused by a crooked shoe. I've seen it many times and it belongs to Cross's horse."

"If so, then why would he be heading north? Twin Creeks is east of here. He should be riding back to the ranch or toward Twin Creeks," reasoned Beck.

"Unless he quit the brand," said Big Jack. "Let's ride into Twin Creeks."

"Are you sure that the boss would approve of us riding into town?"

"I don't give a damn about Baker. I'm tired of hearing about the big bad Morgan Reeves. Come on let's ride."

"I don't like it, I'd rather poke a skunk with a stick than face Reeves," said Luther caustically.

"You are a coward," said Big Jack jeeringly. "Let's git going."

CHAPTER THIRTY-SEVEN

Morgan decided to ride into Twin Creeks before trying to deal with Baker and Big Jack. His first stop, after stabling his horse, was the doctor's office to check on Billy Clay. Tom Clay was in the office when Morgan walked in.

"Hello, Morgan, I see that you are still alive and kicking," greeted Tom.

"Tom, how is Billy doing?"

"He's doing pretty well. Doc says that he'll be up and around in a couple of days. He is eating everything he can find so that is a good sign," replied Tom.

"Where is the doc?"

"He's over at the café, getting something to eat."

"That sounds like a good idea but I'm going to the hotel before anything else."

"I'm sure that she will be glad to see you," Tom said with a smile.

Morgan ignored him, "I'll see you later on."

Morgan left the doctors office and walked to the hotel. Jamie was sitting on the porch.

"Hello Jamie, Where's your mother?"

"Hello, Morgan. She is in her room, I'll get her."

"Thanks, Jamie."

Morgan took a seat on the bench and built a cigarette while waiting for Carla to appear. The door opened and Morgan stood as Carla came out. "Morgan, good to see you again," she said as she took his hand in hers.

"Great to see you too but let's convene at the café, I'm starving."

"Me too," added Jamie.

"I can't argue with both of you," she replied.

The three walked across the street and into the café. They took a seat at one of the tables away from the door. They really had several choices because there were only three other people and two of them were sitting at one table with Doctor Pickard sitting at another. Morgan nodded at the doctor and he nodded back. A middle age woman came over and took their orders and brought back coffee for Morgan and Carla and milk for Jamie.

"Did you visit Billy?" asked Carla.

"I stopped by on the way in. He appears to be doing very well."

"I sat with him too," said Jamie proudly.

"Good boy, Jamie," replied Morgan as he put his hand on the boy's shoulder.

"The food came and the three ate in silence. The doctor paid his bill and came by the table. He nodded at Morgan again and spoke to Carla, "I appreciate your help with young Mr. Clay."

"Glad to do it. Let me know if I can help again."

"I sure will. By the way I understand, Reeves, that you took a bullet in the leg. Stop by the office and I'll take care of it," he answered as he left the café.

Carla looked at Morgan and started to speak but he interrupted. "My leg is fine, it's just a scratch."

She was doubtful but she didn't say anything.

They finished their meal and walked out onto the porch. Morgan stood leaning over the railing of the porch and rolled a cigarette from his Bull Durham sack. He lit it, broke the match and dropped it onto the street. He heard horses coming down the street and glanced up. "That's Big Jack and one of his cronies, is the sheriff around?"

"No, he had to go somewhere and may not be back until tomorrow," replied Jamie.

"You guys stay out of the way," he commanded.

"What are you going to do?" asked Carla.

"Just do what I told you," he snapped as he stepped onto the street.

"That's far enough, Big Jack," snapped Morgan.

"Reeves, you are just the man we are looking for," Big Jack replied.

"You've found me, now get down, both of you," Morgan said harshly.

The two men stepped down and walked in front of their horses. Big Jack looked up and saw Carla. "Well now, I can understand why you are trying to keep her for yourself," said Big Jack with a sneer.

"Keep talking while you can, Big Jack. I'm going to kill you anyway," said Morgan calmly.

"And I'm going to let you try but not with that pistol you are carrying," he replied as he unbuckled his gun belt and allowed it to fall. "Now I'm coming to get you."

Morgan unbuckled his gun belt and handed it back to Carla. "Carla. Take care of these and shoot that bastard if he tries to interfere."

Tom Clay had heard the commotion and came out onto the street. He rushed over to Morgan. "Are you crazy Morg, he'll kill you."

"Tom, you just keep track of that gent that came in with Big Jack."

"Come on, Reeves, I'm tired of waiting," hollered Big Jack.

"You'll be dead for a long time so I think that you would be anxious to live a little longer."

Big Jack shuffled forward and the two men gauged each other. Morgan knew that he was giving away forty or fifty pounds and three or four inches in height but he also knew he had some boxing skills. Big Jack lunged toward Morgan who was expecting it, just not expecting him to be so quick. Big Jack's huge right hand struck him a glancing blow on the side of his head, staggering him. Morgan regained his balance and backed away as Big Jack bored in, swinging from both sides. Morgan stepped in, blocked a right hand, and drove his right hand into Big Jacks ribs. He grunted but kept coming. Morgan backed away and side stepped throwing another right catching him on the side of his head.

The two men backed away and glared at each other. Morgan knew that he needed to take care of Big Jack quickly because his size and weight would wear him down pretty quick. He moved in quickly, hit the big man in his gut with a right hand and then a left to his chin.

Jack's head jerked back and Morgan hit him right on the nose with a right hand. Blood spurted every where including on Morgan.

"You bastard, you broke my nose," the big man yelled.

"That's just the beginning," replied Morgan.

Big Jack rushed foreword but Morgan easily side stepped and clubbed the big man in the back of his head. He stumbled and fell on his face. With an effort, he got up on his knees but Morgan was not going to wait for him to get up. He hit the big man with a thunderous right hand then grabbed him by the hair and drove his knee into his face. Big Jack tried to fall but Morgan held him up and kneed him again and again. He finally let lose of him and Big Jack fell on his face and laid still.

Morgan struggled over to the horse trough and ducked his head into the water. When he raised his head and turned around Big Jack was on his knees holding a pistol.

"Now you bastard, I'm going to kill you," he blubbered through his battered face.

"That does not surprise me. I always thought that you were a coward from the first night that I met you," snapped Morgan.

"I may be a coward but you are going to be dead," he replied as he leveled the pistol.

Morgan heard a shout and saw Tom Clay reaching for his gun. Then he heard three quick shots and saw Big Jack slump to the ground with his face in the dust. He was dead. Morgan looked back at Carla and saw a smoking gun in her hand. He quickly moved over to her side.

Her face didn't show a thing only her eyes were scared and wide open. She was shaking all over. She handed him the Navy Colt and said, "You almost got shot."

"Thanks for saving my bacon," he said.

"I'm . . . I'm sorry. I . . . I had to do it," she cried.

"That's okay Carla, you had more right to kill him than anyone else," he said as he took her in his arms.

Tom Clay came up and looked at Carla then to Morgan. "I got one so both men are dead," he reported.

"Well, looks like Big Jack ran out of luck and Nick Baker is close," replied Morgan.

Jamie walked over and put his arms around Morgan and his mother, "You sure took care of Big Jack, didn't you, Morgan?" said Jamie.

"Yep, Jamie I sure did with some major help from your mother."

"I always knew that ma would take care of him because of what he did to her," he added.

"She is certainly one brave woman," said Tom.

"Thank you, Tom. I think that I want to go to the hotel," said Carla.

"Sure, I'll walk you over there," said Morgan.

"Morg, meet me at the saloon when you get finished," said Tom.

"Give me thirty minutes," replied Morgan.

Morgan took his saddle bags off the horse and escorted Carla and Jamie to the hotel. He spoke to the desk clerk, checked in and then took his belongings up to his room on the second floor. He surveyed the room then left his saddle bags on the bed and found the wash basin. He scrubbed his cut and bruised face and his swollen hands and dried them on a towel. He checked his face in a small mirror and decided that he looked like someone that had been in a fight. He also decided that he needed some new clothes so he would do that before anything else. He left the room, locked it behind him, and headed down the stairs and out of the hotel. He stopped on the sidewalk, rolled a cigarette and dropped the tobacco sack into his vest pocket. He found his matches, lit the cigarette, broke the match and dropped it into the street. He took his time walking over to Tackett's General Store in order to enjoy his smoke and to decide what he would say if Newt Tackett's widow was at the counter.

He dropped the cigarette and crushed it out with his boot and walked inside. Newt Tackett's widow was behind the counter and a middle age woman was paying for her goods. The widow glanced at Morgan and then went back to helping the woman. He looked around and found a couple of shirts and pants that he could wear and waited for the woman to leave the store. When she finally left, Morgan stepped up to the counter and laid the clothes in front of her.

"Hello, Mrs. Tackett."

"Mr. Reeves."

"Mrs. Tackett, I'm sorry about your husband," he said quietly.

"Mr. Reeves, my husband is dead and buried. He was mean and ornery and he was unfaithful to me with several women. Am I sorry that he is dead? I'm not really sure at this point so if I were you I wouldn't spend much time worrying about him."

"Yes, Ma'am, thank you. I need some tobacco also if you don't mind."

She reached back on the shelf and got a sack of tobacco and put it on the counter with the clothing. "Will there be anything else for you, Mr. Reeves?"

"No, Ma'am. That will be all."

"Would you like the clothes wrapped, Mr. Reeves?"

"No, Ma'am, I'm going to wear them as soon as I get to the hotel."

"Very well then," she replied.

He paid for the clothes, picked them up and turned to leave then stopped. "Much obliged, Mrs. Tackett."

"Don't mention it," she replied and Morgan thought that he saw just a hint of a smile come across her face.

He took his new clothing to the hotel, changed and discarded his old clothes. After that he headed to the Red Rooster to meet Tom Clay. When he walked in the door he looked around and saw two men drinking at the bar and Tom sitting at a corner table nursing a beer.

"Hello, Reeves," hollered Cal Daniels from behind the bar. "Need a beer?"

"Sure, and bring my friend here another one, I think that his is dead," replied Morgan.

"Coming right up," hollered the old man.

"Have a seat, Morg. Nice clothes."

"Don't mind if I do and thank you."

"Morg, I've seen you fight but never what you did to Big Jack."

"I had an incentive. He probably would have beaten me nine out of ten times."

"Morg, changing the subject, that Carla is some woman isn't she?"

"She sure is the way she stood up and fought against the mob, and knowing that she and Jamie could have been killed at anytime."

The bartender brought two beers and put them on the table. "Enjoy," he said as he headed back behind the bar.

"Looks like you are fond of Jamie and his mother," Tom said with a smile.

"And you would be right," replied Morgan as he took a long drink from his beer mug.

"Morg, I'd love to have you as a lawman back in Masonville. However, I've heard that the Jackson Ranch is worth a lot of money with the right man to run it."

"What are you trying to tell me, Tom?"

"Well, Billy is going to be laid up for some time and I'm going to need some help, but I do realize that you could have ties to some local folks here."

"Tom, Carla and I have had no conversations about any type of relationship."

"Morg, you can't fool me, that gal is in love with you and I think you are in love with her. Are you concerned about her past?"

"No, of course not, she is a perfect lady."

"Then what is the problem?"

"There is no problem here except that this job is not done. Nick Baker is still out there somewhere."

"You could let the law take care of Baker. Big Jack is the one you really wanted."

"I can't do that."

"Well the job should be over soon. According to Sheriff Billings there couldn't be more than two or three men out there with him."

"I got Garr Madison and Joey Holgram, and Wade Cross apparently left the country so he may not have that many men out there."

"That's even better," said Tom.

"Okay. We'll speak to the sheriff tomorrow when he gets back and we'll ride out there, hopefully with the sheriff.

CHAPTER THIRTY-EIGHT

It was early in the morning and the sheriff was alone, sitting at his desk as Morgan entered. He glanced up, smiled and rocked back in his chair.

"I have to say I'm proud of you, Reeves," said the sheriff.

"And why would that be?" Morgan asked.

"I just wish that I had been here to see that tumble with you and Big Jack. I never thought that I would ever see one man whup him like that," he marveled.

"As you can see, Sheriff, I may have gotten the best of the fight but I still have some bruises that I'll have for quite awhile. Anyway, what about Baker, are we going after him?"

"What do you have in mind?"

"I say you, Tom Clay and I ride out and bring him in. If he doesn't come peaceable we bring him in over his saddle."

"Let's head over to the café and have some breakfast then head out. I don't want to get shot at on an empty stomach," said the sheriff.

"You read my mind," replied Morgan.

The two men headed for the café. They had ordered and were eating before Tom came in. "How's Billy doing?" asked Morgan.

"He's doing much better. Are we riding?" he asked.

"As soon as you fill your belly," replied Morgan.

An hour later the three men were on the way to Nick Baker's Ranch. Morgan filled the sheriff in about the men that he had killed but he was not sure exactly how many men Baker still had at the ranch.

"I know that he has an old man named Henry and another fellow called Herb Slocum. That may be the only men he still has," said the sheriff.

"I'm pretty sure that he has not had time to recruit many extra people," replied Morgan.

"I'd say we just ride in carefully and see if they will surrender," said the sheriff.

"I agree," replied Morgan.

"I have no problem with that either," added Tom.

When the three men reached the wooden bridge they halted and looked around. No men or horses were in sight. They rode across the bridge, spread out and waited. No sounds could be heard.

"Baker, come on out," hollered Morgan.

They waited several minutes and then Morgan hollered again, "Baker, come on out or we'll come in and get you."

After several more minutes Morgan took out the Henry, fired several shots over the house.

"Don't shoot," hollered a man that came out of the front door with his hands above his head.

"That's Henry," said the sheriff. "He's harmless."

"Keep walking, Henry," hollered Morgan.

"I don't have a gun," he hollered back.

Henry walked up to the three men. "Sheriff, Mr. Baker rode off three or four hours ago. There is nobody here except me."

"Where is Slocum?" asked the sheriff.

"He rode out with Baker."

"Now what do we do?" asked Tom.

"We follow him to where we don't know or let him go and hope that he doesn't come back," answered the sheriff.

"John, do you know anything about where Baker came from?" asked Morgan.

"He was pretty tight lipped but I believe that he came from somewhere in Kansas."

"I'd suggest that we ride back to town. I know that Carla believes that Baker shot her husband or had some one do it but from what I understand, there is not much evidence," he suggested.

"Unfortunately, I don't think that there is any evidence," replied the sheriff.

"Henry, I'd suggest that you stay in the barn," advised Morgan. "Let's get back to town."

The three men turned and rode out in the direction of town. When they were sure that they were out of sight of the ranch Morgan held up his hand and the three men reined in. Morgan dismounted and the other two men followed suit. He pulled out his sack of Bull Durham, rolled a cigarette and passed it around. After all of them had lit up the sheriff spoke, "Morgan I don't understand, why we are leaving, what's going on?"

"I can tell you what's going on," replied Tom Clay. "There was a rifle barrel pointed through that front window."

"But Henry said that Baker had ridden out three or four hours ago."

"Sheriff, I know that you know Henry better than we do. Did you see any differences in him," asked Morgan.

The sheriff scratched his chin and replied, "Well, he did seem a mite nervous."

"And that mite nervousness was because the gun was pointed directly at his back," replied Morgan.

"So you think that Baker is still inside and that is why you suggested Henry stay in the barn."

"That's exactly right," responded Morgan.

"So how are we going to get them out?" asked Tom.

"I figure that within thirty minutes I can get behind the house. I want you two to wait the thirty minutes then ride within shouting range and call Baker out. Also I don't want you to get too close until I get situated. After you call out a couple of times I want you to put as many bullets that you can in the house."

"We can do that with pleasure, can't we?" the sheriff spoke to Tom.

"You bet I'm sure that we can handle it," replied Tom.

"And by the way, keep your eyes open he may try and leave this direction," added Morgan.

"Okay, let's do it," said Tom.

"I'm going to leave my horse here and go in on foot so tie him and I'll pick him up later," Morgan said as he walked toward the house.

When he reached the creek, Morgan dropped into it and walked several yards until he could come up the creek bank behind the bunk house. He assumed that Baker and his men, whatever the number was, would be in the ranch house. He ran through a clearing and found cover behind the barn. He was quite sure that Old Henry was still in the barn and he hoped that he wouldn't make any noise. He looked at his watch. It had taken him twenty minutes. He had about twenty-five to thirty yards to get behind the house and it was all open fields. He either could run quickly and cover the distance and hope that no one in the house would see him or try and crawl. He decided to take a chance and run.

He pulled the Navy Colt, held it in his right hand and ran. He had only covered about half of the distance when he stepped in a hole wrenching his ankle. Now it was going to be tough he thought. His ankle was already swelling when he pulled off his neckerchief and quickly wrapped it up. It was going to be painful but he had to do it. He stood up and hobbled as quickly as he could until he reached the corner of the house.

He stood for a few moments leaning against the building and he heard the sheriff call out for Baker. "Come on out, Baker, we know that you are in there."

Then rifle shots blazed away toward the two men. "Come in and get as, Billings, if you want us that badly."

"That's exactly what we plan to do," replied Sheriff Billings.

Morgan leaned on the wall of the house and walked to the back door. He put his ear to the door but he couldn't hear anything. With the Navy Colt in his right hand he tried the door with his left. The door opened a crack and he saw two men at the window in front of the house. From what he had heard, the other man must be Herb Slocum.

On his sore and bruised knees Morgan crawled inside the house and quietly moved toward the front of the house. Bullets were flying everywhere; Baker and Slocum were concentrating on the sheriff and Tom Clay and forgot to pay attention to the back door.

"Drop the guns, Gents, or die," Morgan hollered over the noise of the gunfire.

They both turned their heads toward Morgan.

"If you are planning what I think that you are planning you are sealing your fate in boot hill," snapped Morgan.

"I don't think that you can get us both," replied Baker.

"It's your choice," countered Morgan calmly.

They both turned simultaneously and aimed at Morgan.

Morgan emptied the Navy Colt into the two men before they could get off a single shot. He emptied the cylinder of the colt and put in fresh bullets then crawled toward the two men. They were both dead. The sheriff and Tom Clay were still firing into the house.

"Tom, Sheriff, hold your fire."

The bullets still came at a rapid pace. "Hold your fire," Morgan hollered louder and finally the shooting stopped.

"Are you okay, Morg?" asked Tom.

"I'm fine, they are both dead. Come on in," replied Morgan.

The two men came through the door and looked at the two dead men on the floor.

"Looks like you got them both," said Tom.

"Yep, it looks like we are finished here," replied Morgan.

"Let's get us a wagon and haul these two gents to town," said the sheriff.

Morgan hobbled toward the front door. "Say, are you shot?" asked Tom.

"No, I stepped in a hole as I was running toward the house and I sprained my ankle."

"Morg, you would do anything to get some sympathy," laughed Tom.

"Actually, I did that so that I wouldn't have to carry these bodies out of this house," he replied as he limped through the door with a smile on his face.

"At least we were thoughtful enough to bring your horse so that you didn't have to walk a quarter mile," countered Tom.

Chapter Thirty-nine

The three men rode into town with Henry driving the wagon carrying the two bodies. They stopped in front of the undertaker's office and had to clear away the crowd before they could unload the bodies.

"I'm going to check on Billy and then I'll need a drink. Gents, how about us meeting at the Red Rooster to celebrate," said Tom.

"I've got some paperwork to finish before I can do anything else. I'll try and meet you in an hour or so if you are still there," replied the sheriff.

"We'll probably still be there," declared Tom.

"John, part of this paperwork does not have anything to do with a resignation would it?" asked Morgan.

"Nope, I have decided to keep this badge for the next eight months and then allow the voters to decide whether or not they want me around," explained the sheriff.

"I think that would be the best idea," replied Tom. "I'll talk to you both later on."

"Sheriff, if you need any information from me just holler. I'm heading for the hotel," said Morgan.

"I don't think that I will but if I do I know where to find you. By the way, you could do much worst than to marry that woman. She has some good land with water and it could be a very successful ranch with the right help."

"Thanks, Sheriff, but she has not given any indication that she wants anything to do with me," replied Morgan.

"I hate to say this but you're a damn fool if you don't ask her," said the sheriff.

Morgan looked at the sheriff, turned and walked to the hotel. He stopped at the desk and asked for Carla.

"Mr. Reeves, she and Jamie rented a buggy and rode out to the ranch. I told her that I didn't think that it was a good idea but she wanted to do it," he said.

"She is a stubborn woman sometimes," Morgan replied with a smile. "You probably could not have stopped her anyway."

He took his key and went up to his room. He changed his shirt, washed up and went to the saloon to meet Tom, who was on his second beer when Morgan walked in.

"How's Billy?"

"Doc says that if he continues to progress the way he's is doing now he'll be ready to ride back home in a week or so."

The bartender brought him a beer, "You wash up pretty good Mr. Reeves," said Cal as he winked at Tom.

"I can remember when Morg here was a snappy dresser," said Tom with a smile.

"Drink your beer and close your mouth," growled Morgan.

"You are upset because your woman rode out and left you," teased Cal.

"Number one, she is not my woman and why are you trying to keep tabs on her you old goat," replied Morgan gruffly.

The swinging doors opened and in walked sheriff Billings. "There is a buggy coming down the street."

"What's the matter, Sheriff, haven't you ever seen a buggy before?" said Morgan.

"Sure I seen plenty of buggies but not one like this with such a beautiful woman driving it," remarked Billings.

Morgan drained his beer glass, stood up and walked out the door. The bartender looked at Tom, "He was in such a hurry he left his tab for you to pay."

"Barkeep, that wouldn't be the first time but I'll be glad to pay," replied Tom as he left some coins on the table and followed the sheriff out of the saloon.

Carla saw Morgan, stopped the buggy and waited for Morgan to help her down. Morgan stared at her for a long moment.

"Something wrong?" she asked.

"No, no. I was just looking at the most beautiful woman that I've ever seen."

She blushed, "Are you going to help me down or do I need to ask someone else to help me," she pouted.

Morgan quickly walked to the buggy and helped her down. He held her close for a moment and she didn't attempt to move away.

"How was the ranch?" asked the sheriff.

"The barn and the bunk house are still standing but the house is completely destroyed," she replied.

"We found some pictures," volunteered Jamie. He pulled out a little tin box that was blackened from the fire. "See."

"That's great, Jamie, maybe we can look at them later," replied Morgan.

"Mrs. Jackson, I know that I have made many mistakes and have been nasty to you but I hope that you will forgive me. I also hope that you are planning to rebuild," replied the sheriff.

"Yes, I am planning to rebuild and I'll need somebody," she said. "I'll not just need anybody, but somebody that can and will help with the building and hire a new crew that can put this ranch back on an operating basis." She looked at Morgan, "Will you stay, Morgan?"

Morgan sensed the loneliness and maybe despair that she was feeling when she spoke. Carla had been by herself except for Jamie for two years and she had held up very well but then she had the hatred of people like Nick Baker and Newt Tackett to keep her going. What would she do now? She seemed desperate to believe in something or someone. That could be a start for them.

"Carla, I'll stay as long as you want me too."

Tom Clay smiled and slapped Morgan on the shoulder, "You are smarter than I thought you were. Congratulations, Pardoner."

"That's just what I was thinking," said the sheriff as he grabbed Morgan's hand and shook it.

Jamie ran over and hugged Morgan, "I'm sure glad that you are staying."

"Me too, Jamie," he said as he patted the boy on his shoulder.

"Jamie, why don't you come over to the jail, I have some things to show you and tell you about," said the sheriff.

"I'd love to do that," Jamie replied happily.

"Sheriff, I'm going with you," said Tom and the three walked down to the jail.

Carla took Morgan's hand, "I'm really glad that you are going to stay."

"Me too," he replied.

There was much more he wanted to say, but it was too soon. Too much had happened. There would be time enough to tell her the rest when she was ready to hear it. There would be all the time in the world for both of them.